WOLF CALLED

FORTITUDE WOLVES - BOOK ONE

NICOLE R. TAYLOR

O*nce upon a time...*
That's how stories like this usually began, didn't they?

Snow White and the Huntsman. A monster at the door, desperate to eat grandma. Three little pigs trying to thwart the Big Bad Wolf. A father searching for his child and a mother doing everything in her power to keep her from him. A wicked witch and a dark prince.

Power, blood, and sacrifice.

And a foolish girl, in over her head, finding out she wasn't normal.

I lay on the ground, my hair ratty and splayed out beneath me. The ochre dirt of the outback was still warm from the day's sun, the grit digging into my naked flesh.

Numb. Bruised. *Alive.*

The stars of the Milky Way dusted across the sky,

reaching from horizon to horizon. In the distance, I could hear the crash of waves against the cliffside and the roar of the wind as it flew across the ocean and up over the ragged rocks.

I'd never seen or heard like this before. A switch had been flipped inside me, and now everything was in high definition. The sludge called life I'd been wading through had been transformed into clear, crisp, crystal.

Understanding.

I'd been fooling myself. Pretending I was harsh and abrasive like heavy duty sandpaper, full to bursting with bravado that won me no friends and gained me plenty of enemies.

It was a mask I'd slapped over the truth.

"Sloane!"

I heard my name over the howling wind and sat up. My hair covered my naked breasts and I shivered, my humanity flooding back in a nauseating wave.

"*Sloane!*"

The wind turned, driving towards me, and I drew in a deep breath. That's when I smelt it for the first time.

Blood, shadow, death.

Vampire.

CHAPTER 1

SLOANE

I was thirteen when I started dreaming about the full moon.

Some people would say it's an unlucky number, that it foretold bad karma coming my way. Too bad I didn't believe in prophecies, let alone the supernatural. The moon was constant, and now it was a friend in the sky, a comfort to a lone wolf hiding from a dark past.

The sound of a crashing glass broke me out of my daze, and I blinked. A group of men roared at the big screen TV across the pub, shouting at the replay of their team being slaughtered by the opposition—a contested goal on the second quarter siren.

I stood behind the bar, a damp tea towel in hand, and sighed. It was just another Friday night during AFL season.

Nestled in the port city of Fremantle, Western Australia, the *Sailor's Arms* was the cheapest and closest pub to the docks, which had been the lifeblood of the southern part of the Perth metro area for generations. It meant the clientele was mostly male and mostly stevedores—hard men with dangerous jobs.

They piled in after their shifts to get drunk, watch the footy, have the occasional union meeting, and organise the odd picket line. Most of them were reluctant to go home to their wives and kids, lingering for hours on end until the bouncer peeled them off their stools and kicked them out. It wasn't a Friday night unless someone threw a punch—or any night of the week for that matter.

It definitely wasn't how I wanted to spend my nights, but in this day and age, a job was a job. Especially when a person needed an employer who didn't ask too many questions.

"Hey, Sloane," a voice said behind me. "How's it going?"

Turning, I smiled as my one and only friend approached. Times were lonely when one's life was reduced to a fake identity.

I died a little inside from jealousy every time I saw Yvette. She was tall, leggy, blonde with big blue eyes, and got all the tips and then some. Often underestimated because of her looks, her confidence and resilience were boundless—the former something I sorely lacked—and it was all for her three-year-old daughter Brittany. She worked in this seedy place and picked up extra shifts at two other jobs, her hours based around her kid's schooling. I never understood how she managed it all, but somehow, she did. That was some superhero magic if I ever saw it. I could barely manage myself, let alone a tiny human.

"It goes," I replied. "Same chaos, different day."

"How's the depth?" She flashed me a wink.

"Above the flood marker. Worst in fifty years, they say."

"Oh, don't be so dramatic." She tied a knot in the bottom of her T-shirt so she could show off her trim midriff. "It isn't that bad. Hector pays us and doesn't keep the tip jar."

"Yay," I drawled. "At least there's always the jar."

"What have you done to your hair, girl?" Reaching out, she grabbed the long braid that'd fallen forwards over my shoulder and tugged.

"Ow! That hurts, you know." I cursed and complained as Yvette undid my hair. Once it was loose, she combed her fingers through my long, almost black locks, fluffing them up.

"There," she said, "much better. You're much prettier when you wear your hair out. You should put a little gloss on your lips, too." She grabbed me again and tied the hem of my T-shirt into a knot like hers. The material rode up, exposing my stomach, and I flushed.

"*Yvette*," I complained.

"There. That's so much better." She stood back and

gave me the once-over. "You've got a hot bod, Sloane. You might actually get a few tips from the rabble, or a free drink at least." She eyed me and tried to fight a smile from pulling at her lips. "*Say it.*"

I rolled my eyes and slumped my shoulders. "Thanks, Yvette."

Her smile widened and she pulled pint glasses out of the dishwasher. "Hey, did you do your exams yet? How'd they go?"

I shook my head. "Next week."

She beamed at me. "Look at you, *university girl*. All by computer, too."

I shrugged. "It's a real slog. I'm not sure if I'm gunna pass."

Between shifts at the pub, I had a heavy course load and no one to help me with it. No study group, no teacher's assistant, no lectures. Just an ancient laptop, the Wi-Fi at the local fast-food joint, and my brain to piece it all together.

Trying to get a university degree online sucked, but I didn't have the time or money to go in person. I had to make do with whatever I could afford. Besides, it was much easier to enroll with a fake ID on the internet—no one checked your picture.

"You will," Yvette said. "Just wait."

Motion in my peripheral caught my attention, and I turned to serve a customer who'd leaned against the bar. When my gaze collided with the man standing behind me, I nearly choked on my spit. He was my type, which was a rarity around here.

Rough, devilish, iridescent eyes, messy hair, leather jacket, strong shoulders—the works. This guy checked off all items on my list and topped it off with a stubbled jaw, a tattoo peeking out the top of his T-shirt, and direct eye contact. The perfect man...*on paper.*

My heart fluttered for a split-second before I composed myself, shutting off all traces of spark. Life was complicated enough as it was without adding the constant disappointment of dating to the mix. Truth was, I didn't have the time.

"Sloane," the man said, looking me over. "*That's* what you call yourself?"

My expression faded. "Excuse me?"

He tilted his head to the side. "It's nice."

I frowned, my heart skipping a beat, and his lips quirked as if he'd heard the change in tempo.

"Can I get you a drink?" *Best hurry this up.*

The man stared at me, his hazel eyes burning a hole right through me. I squirmed and swallowed hard.

"Are you going to order something?" I asked. "I've got other customers waiting."

The man looked down the empty bar and raised his eyebrow. "Slow night, huh?"

"There's a lull right now," I fired back. I pointed to the big screen TV across the pub that was showing tonight's AFL match between the Pies and the Dockers. "Third quarter just started."

The man followed my finger and rolled his eyes.

Down the bar where Yvette was pulling a beer for an *actual* customer, she met my gaze and mouthed, *Are you okay?*

I nodded, hoping I wouldn't regret it.

"I don't want a drink," the man said, leaning forwards. "I'm here for your protection."

"W. T. F," I scoffed. "That's a good one. You? Protect me? Worst pick-up line ever." I turned to walk away, but his hand shot out and grasped my arm, his cold fingers biting into my skin. "*Let me go.*"

"Your father sent me," he murmured.

My heart literally stopped beating for what felt like a full minute. My so-called father had never shown interest in me once in my entire life. Not even when my mum died did he put up his hand to take on his fatherly duties. I'd been shipped off to foster care, and good thing, too. He was a criminal, and a notorious one at that, which was why I'd done everything in my power to disappear.

I wanted nothing to do with him. *Nothing at all.*

Wrenching my arm away, I snarled, "I don't have a father."

The man's eyes darkened. "He'd beg to differ."

Why? What did he want with me? The thought flashed through my mind like a bolt of lightning.

Looking at the guy in front of me, I tried to weigh my options, but he wasn't about to let me.

His eyes narrowed. "If I can find you, then so can they."

"They?" I scowled, annoyed by the vagueness of it all. "What is it this time? Was it an expansion job that's turned into a turf war? Did he try to steal someone else's corner by the local milk bar so he could sell his little packets of powder? I know how these things go. Revenge begets revenge, and that revenge begets more revenge. Why do you think I want nothing to do with him? *He wasn't my father*. At least, he wasn't the one I needed."

"Still, he is and—"

"Look, whatever your name is..." I waved my hand at him.

"Chaser."

I snorted. "*Really?* That's your name?"

His eyes narrowed in warning. "This isn't a joke."

"*It never is.*"

"Is everything okay here?"

I glanced at Yvette, who'd approached when things had become heated. We had a code behind the bar. When things got tense, check in. If things got out of hand, call in brute force. We had a zero-tolerance policy in place for a reason.

"Yeah," I said, not breaking eye contact with Chaser. "He was just leaving."

"You'll regret it," he said, not even glancing at Yvette. "It's bad this time."

"It's bad *every* time," I shot back, "and I'm not interested."

"Do I need to get Bobby?" Yvette asked, glaring at Chaser. Bobby was the bouncer, otherwise known as the one-man brute force security squad.

I pointed towards the exit. "*He was just leaving.*"

Chaser held up his hands and smirked. His lip pulled up on one side more than the other, giving him a devilish allure.

"No need," he said. "I can take myself."

Chaser shoved his hands into the pockets of his leather jacket and strode through the pub like he owned the joint. People—who I knew were their own special breed of violent—stepped out of the way to let him through, which didn't bode well. Other dogs knew when to bow to an alpha.

"What was that about?" Yvette asked, her forehead creasing. "Is everything good with you?"

"It's nothing." I didn't dare look away, worried if I lost sight of him, he'd double back and go for round two.

"Didn't look like nothing."

Just as Chaser was about to walk through the exit, he glanced over his shoulder. His gaze caught mine, and he smirked. Turning my back, I knew it wouldn't be the last time he graced me with his presence.

Yvette gave me a ride home after the pub closed for the night.

I usually took a bus and walked a couple of blocks in the dark, but she wouldn't let me go by myself, not after the altercation with Chaser. I could look after myself, but I didn't argue.

Yvette's little red Suzuki Swift zoomed across the bridge near the docks and into the suburbs, bouncing along the road. The orange glow of streetlights flashed overhead as the radio blared some top-40 pop song. Not my taste in music, but driver's choice.

I barely listened as she filled me in on her daughter's latest school report and the in-depth account of the little girl's gold-starred artwork.

I stared at the three-quarter moon rearing over the city, my mind uneasy. My father had sent Chaser to find me, which meant I hadn't done a good job of hiding. A fake ID was no longer going to cut it. He knew where I worked and would soon dig up my address...if he hadn't already.

What did he want? Had my life been threatened by his enemies? Or did he need me to do something for him? Had to be one of the two. Either way, something big was going down and I had to cover my tracks.

I'd hardly registered the trip when Yvette pulled up in front of my building. She let the engine idle as I jerked upright.

The apartment block was a mid-rise, made from what felt like one continuous slab of concrete that was cast and set in the 1970s, otherwise known as the land that soundproofing forgot. It was a complete dump—five stories with twenty apartments—but the rent was cheap, and it had an entrance that gave the illusion of security with its coded fob system. All I had to do was press the tag against the sensor and the lock would click open.

"Sloane..." Yvette worried her bottom lip, then turned to face me. "Are you sure everything's okay?"

"Yeah." I shrugged. "Why wouldn't it be?"

"That guy grabbed you and you just shrugged it off. It would've rattled me."

I breathed deeply as a sharp pang of anger threatened. "What was I supposed to do?" I asked her. "I'm not going to cry about it. He wanted a reaction, and I wasn't going to give it to him. He knew it, so he moved on. That was it."

"But—"

"You know what guys are like in that place," I said, fishing in my pocket. I peeled out a five-dollar bill and handed it to her. "For some petrol."

"Oh, Slo, you don't have to."

"I know, but I want to." I smiled and folded her fingers around the pink plastic note. "Thanks for the lift."

She looked me over with a frown as I opened the car door. "You call if you need anything, okay?"

"Sure." I hopped out and waved as I crossed the footpath. I totally wasn't going to, but if it put her mind at ease...

Yvette waited until I was inside before she pulled away, the Suzuki Swift taking off down the street like a red bullet.

Hightailing it up the stairwell, I reached the fifth floor and pushed out into the hallway. The sound of televisions cranked all the way up and the odd bark of a dog echoed through the concrete as I made my way to my flat. Rounding the corner, I came to a screeching halt when I saw Mrs. Adelstein at her door.

She was wearing her usual getup, which consisted of a fluffy pink dressing gown and matching slippers. Tonight, she had purple rollers in her greying hair, and her wrinkly hand was clutching her dressing gown together over her chest.

Mrs. Adelstein was a selective agoraphobic. She didn't like to go outside the apartment block but revelled in the business of everyone who lived in it. I was sure she had notebooks filled with surveillance on all her neighbours, including me. All that was missing was her tinfoil hat.

"You're home early," she said, glaring at me. Obviously, I'd messed up her timetable.

"I got a lift from a friend," I replied, stepping around her.

"I see. That's good. It's not good for a young woman to be out after dark." She clucked her tongue. "The news is bad these days. Always a story about a girl being murdered or...*you-know-what*." She shook her head and one of her rollers came loose. "Terrible. *Terrible*."

"I'm fine, Mrs. Adelstein." I slipped past and unlocked the door.

She coughed loudly, then shuffled back to her flat. "No, no, no," she muttered. "It's *them* you have to worry about."

Making a face, I glanced down the hall and darted inside as the last lock clicked open. Mrs. Adelstein needed to wrap some foil through those rollers, *stat*.

The door closed behind me, and I pressed my back against the wood, my fingers fumbling for the deadlock. Safe at last...but I knew it was only an illusion.

It was time to think about leaving. *Again*.

CHAPTER 2
SLOANE

As predicted, things got weird the next night, and it had nothing to do with the football on the big screen.

My shift got off to a good start when I scored a ten-dollar tip—which I shoved down my bra so I would get to keep it—but when the place filled up, it raised my anxiety levels.

Even after all this time, old habits died hard. My gaze darted around the bar, looking for threats where there were none.

Seven years, I thought. *Nothing for seven years, and now...*

It'd always been a possibility that my father might try to find me, but I knew how to handle myself. Growing up in a rough neighbourhood, followed by my awkward teenage years being dominated by a constant rotation of less-than-stellar foster homes, had instilled a ruthless survival instinct in me. Sometimes it almost felt animalistic—like a predator would protect its food and territory—and it always made me think of him. *My father*, the ultimate predator.

The night wore on, and in the darkest and dingiest corner of the *Sailor's Arms*, I spotted a familiar face.

Chaser.

How long had he been sitting there?

Yvette sidled up beside me. "You just saw him, too, huh?"

I nodded and tried to keep my hands busy. They were trembling and they never trembled.

"He's not even watching the game," she went on. "And he's ignoring all those flirty women. At least three have tried it on since I noticed him sitting there." She glanced at me.

"And you think he's waiting for *me* to flirt with *him*?" I snorted. "Fat chance."

Yvette frowned. "Why do you keep saying things like that, Slo?"

"Things like what?" I picked up a rag and wiped down the bar, anything to not look at her.

"He grabbed you," she said with a shake of her head. "If that was flirting, then I'd run the other way."

"He won't do it again if he knows what's good for him."

"He's looking again."

Curiosity got the better of me, and I glanced up.

Sure enough, Chaser was nursing a bottle of beer,

his gaze sweeping the room, but it wasn't focused on the football game or the women casting him flirty glances. He was sizing up the men. Every once in a while he would glance towards the entrance, then over to the bar where Yvette and I were staring at him.

"Oh, shit," Yvette said, spinning around. "Do you think he saw us?"

"Yeah," I drawled, giving Chaser the biggest stink-eye I could muster. "He saw us all right."

She worried her bottom lip. "He's starting to worry me."

I tensed and draped the rag back across the edge of the sink. Harassing me was one thing—I could handle a little heat—but when it screwed with Yvette's sense of safety, I saw red.

"I'll be right back," I said, waving her off when she tried to stop me.

Rounding the end of the bar, I strode across the pub, ignoring the sidelong glances, and stopped in front of a smug-looking Chaser. He wanted a confrontation, so here it was.

Snatching the beer bottle out of his hand, I glared at him with as much force as I could muster.

"I wasn't finished with that," he complained.

"You're hogging the table," I declared. "And I can guarantee your beer is flat. You may as well be drinking toilet water."

He lounged back in the booth. "He warned me about this."

"Excuse me?" I felt my cheeks redden and thanked God we were in the corner where it was dark so he couldn't see.

"You're a handful. Can see it already."

Holding up the bottle, I tipped the beer into his lap. "How's that for a wet patch?"

People around us snickered as Chaser held out his hands in mock defeat.

"There are worse things in the world."

I tossed the empty beer bottle at him.

He caught it against his chest and laughed. It was the wrong thing to do, but luckily for him, there was a table between us.

"Get out of my face, Chaser," I snarled. "Go back to my father and tell him the same words I told him seven years ago when he sent another loser like you after me. I'd rather asphyxiate on my own vomit than lay eyes on him ever again. *He doesn't exist to me.* You got it?"

Turning on my heel, I stalked across the pub, seething so hard I almost spontaneously combusted. When I calmed down enough to check if Chaser was still there or not, the booth was empty.

Good. He was bad for my health.

***

Stuffing a hot chip into my mouth, I chewed and thumped out another sentence. My poor laptop.

My nights often went like this. Go to the local fast-food restaurant. Order the cheapest meal they had. Commandeer a table for a minimum of two to three hours. Then pack as much course work in as I could before walking the five blocks home in the dark, looking as tough as I could so I wouldn't be attacked. *Hopefully*. My computer was a relic of a bygone era, but twenty bucks was twenty bucks around here.

I'd become a regular fixture after six months. Management eventually twigged I was trying to study and didn't hassle me anymore. I took up as little space as possible and kept away during the dinnertime rush, so we'd come to a silent understanding. As long as I wasn't running drugs to their customers or casing the joint to prepare for an armed robbery, they didn't mind me hanging out.

Renee worked the counter on Sunday, Monday, and Wednesday nights when I came in to study. She was an eighteen-year-old who served me my usual order of cheeseburger, fries, and a Coke for several weeks before something mysterious shifted in the air, and she started to sit with me during her breaks. Two unlikely acquaintances.

Tonight, she was watching me type and flip through my notes, her eyebrows in a constant state of interest.

"What do you do when you come in here?" she asked. "Are you writing a book or something?"

"Hardly," I replied. "I'm writing a political science essay."

"You go to school on your computer?" She stared at the lid of my laptop like it was the doorway to Narnia.

"Yeah. It will take a billion years and a billion dollars, but you can do it. At least the Wi-Fi here is free."

"What do you want to be?"

"I'm not entirely sure yet, but right now, I'd settle for educated."

Renee snorted and took a chip from my tray.

"You don't want to go to uni?" I asked.

"Can't afford it," she replied, then took out her phone. It clicked as she unlocked it, and her thumb flicked as she began scrolling.

"There's government help for that, you know."

She shrugged. "Too dumb."

"No one is too dumb for school," I shot back. "I bet you could do it."

She gave me a look and went back to scrolling on her phone.

I glanced to the side as a man walked past with a tray and narrowed my eyes. I'd been jumpy ever since Chaser showed up at the pub, carrying the latest sob story from father dearest. He wanted to protect me? From what?

This is probably Dad's plan, I thought. *Install a seed of doubt into his only daughter and she'll come back to the compound for protection.* I wasn't going to fall for it.

Watching the man, I decided I didn't like the look of him. He was wearing a black bomber jacket, dark shirt, and dark pants—the three most common clothing items in a police identikit.

He was rough around the edges, but who wasn't in this neighbourhood? Hell, they had an armed security guard at a family restaurant once the sun went down. There was an indicator of the clientele right there.

Still, I snapped the lid of my laptop closed and gathered my notes, shoving the lot into my battered backpack.

"You going?" Renee asked.

"Yeah, you want the rest of these fries?"

She grabbed the edge of the tray and slid it towards her.

"See ya," she muttered, shoving a fry into her mouth, her gaze barely leaving her phone.

"See you later."

There was no further reply, and I rolled my eyes. *Kids and their phones.*

Sliding my backpack on, I pushed out of the restaurant and stepped onto the footpath.

Glancing over my shoulder, I sank deeper into my denim jacket and lengthened my stride. Crossing the road, I threw another look at the golden arches behind me. The door opened, and bomber jacket man appeared.

My heart skipped a beat, and I fished around in my pocket for my keys. Shoving a key through each finger, I fashioned myself a pointy set of brass knuckles just in case I had to stab and run.

I put my head down and hurried down the footpath, passing under orange streetlights and darting across side streets. I was a shadow in a shadowy world.

Looking back over my shoulder every so often, I saw the man walking at a distance. I couldn't be sure he was following me—there was a chance he was just going the same direction—but I couldn't be too careful.

My heartbeat sped up and I put my head down, increasing my speed. I was on the verge of running, but I held on to my nerves with everything I had.

I rounded the last corner before I reached my street and caught sight of home in the distance. I'd never been happier to see the dump in my entire life, and I hurried towards it, stepping into the ring of light surrounding the concrete monstrosity.

Throwing one last look back, the man was nowhere to be seen, but my heart didn't stop thundering in my chest. Slamming the fob against the sensor, I was granted access. Pushing through the door, I closed it behind me and heaved a sigh of relief. *Safe and sound for now.*

When I reached the fifth floor, Mrs. Adelstein was lurking in the hallway again.

"It's late," she said when she saw me.

The only way was past her, so I sidled by and flashed her a fake smile. "I was studying."

"Oh, that's right. It's Monday."

She didn't seem to be interested in chatting, so

knowing what was good for me, I kept walking. Fishing out my keys, I let them fall from between my fingers and shoved the first one into the deadlock.

"Sloane?" she called out, signalling she'd had an afterthought.

Rolling my eyes, I plastered on a smile before I turned around. "Yes?"

"There was someone knocking on your door earlier."

"Oh?" I froze, the smile twitching on my face.

"He was loud. Next time, tell him to knock a little softer."

A bad feeling crawled up and down my spine. "Who was he?"

"A mean-looking man," she went on. "Leather jacket, boots. He knocked and knocked, and I told him to get lost. You better not be mixed up in the drugs. A smart girl like you...?" She clucked her tongue and shuffled back into her apartment. She went inside and slammed the door behind her, the sound echoing like thunder down the concrete hallway.

Leather jacket and big boots? Was it Chaser...or someone else? More importantly, how did he get into the building?

Swallowing hard, I undid the second lock and slipped inside my apartment, making sure all the locks were in place before latching the chain. I turned on the lights and flipped the sofa back. Reaching inside the lining, my fingers brushed past springs and stuffing before they rubbed up against what I was looking for.

Taking out the 9mm handgun and the box of matching bullets, I sat on the floor and loaded the magazine, listening to the sounds of the apartment block. A kid screamed, television noise roared through the wall, a door slammed, muffled voices argued, and a telephone rang.

If Chaser was right and someone was coming for me, then I'd be ready. And if Chaser came back... Well, I wasn't sure what I would do if he turned up again. He hadn't gotten the message last night if Mrs. Agoraphobic down the hall was handing in her report.

I just wanted to be left alone. Was that too much to ask? *Seemed like it.*

I'd put all this behind me years ago. I was getting on with life, and even though things weren't amazing, they were better than they ever could've been if the powers-that-be had let my father take custody.

Out here, in the real world, I was a human being. Back there, back in Melbourne, I was a commodity—a bargaining chip with a bleak future. There was nothing else for the daughter of a criminal kingpin to be.

If I kept refusing Chaser's advances, there was no doubt in my mind he would try to take me by force. When the moment came, I'd have to be ready. No hesitation.

No one gained their freedom by hiding their head in the sand. No one at all.

Slamming the full magazine into the handgrip of the gun, I made sure the safety was on and glanced at the door. I would put a bullet right in Chaser's pretty boy face before he took me anywhere.

He could count on it.

CHAPTER 3

SLOANE

Jack and Coke. Three shots of Fireball Whisky. Two craft beers. Five shots of Jägermeister. A round of Carlton Draught.

Glancing at the clock on the wall, I narrowed my eyes. Yvette was late. *Again.*

More beer and some Jack and Coke. Fireball, Fireball, Fireball. *Strawberry vodka lemonade.*

"Hey, Slo," Yvette said as she appeared from out back. "Busy night?"

"Yeah," I shot at her. "I can hardly keep up."

"Sorry," she said with a pout. "Brittany had a meltdown right before I was leaving. Brown stuff was *everywhere.*" She made a puking motion.

I suppressed an eye roll and flung a dishcloth at her.

She caught it against her chest and laughed. "Thanks, Slo."

"I let you take advantage of me more often than I should."

"Aw, don't be like that." Yvette wrapped her arms around my neck, giving me a faceful of her favourite lilac perfume. "I'll give you some of my tips for the cover. You know I'm good for it."

"And you know I will say keep it because you need the extra nappies."

Yvette leaned against the bar and crossed her arms over her chest. "Hey, I uh... I spotted that guy on my way in."

I screwed up my face, not hearing her over the music. "Huh?"

"That guy is here," she repeated. "The one whose *you-know-what* you gave a beer shower to."

A group of men at the bar sniggered, and I suppressed the urge to give them a piece of my mind. Those creeps were nothing compared to the things a man like Chaser was capable of. Too bad I wasn't allowed to bring a gun to work, though it was sitting pretty in my bag out back. One thing they didn't do here was a security check on their staff, and that was good for me—especially since it was against the law to carry.

"You're kidding me," I said, my gaze flickering around the pub.

"If I didn't know any better, I would think he has a thing for you," Yvette said, nodding across the room.

"Be careful, Slo. You know what happened the last time someone here got themselves a stalker."

Did I ever. Harriet was one of the good ones. She had been sweet, innocent, and was just trying to get by in the world like the rest of us. Problem was, she had a bleeding heart and gave more than she ought to. Harriet wasn't with us anymore in the most permanent way possible.

"Can you hold down the bar for ten?" I asked, wiping my hands on my jeans.

"You're not going to talk to him again, are you?" she asked, looking alarmed. "I know I said—"

"I know what you said," I shot back. "Don't worry about it."

She glanced over at Chaser again and shrugged, signalling she either didn't know what to say or didn't want to get involved. Couldn't say I blamed her, what with her little girl at home and all. She didn't want to become a statistic, but I had little to lose.

"Slo!" Yvette called out.

"It'll be fine." I waved her off and rounded the end of the bar.

Wandering through the press of men in high-vis work gear gathered for the latest stevedores union meeting, I searched for Chaser. Knowing he would be in the darkest corner possible with the best vantage point, I made for the row of booths he'd been sitting in the other night.

Sure enough, he was in the same one, lounging like

he owned the place with his arm slung over the back of the padded seat.

I didn't like it. He looked cold and calculating—a different kind of predatory I hadn't encountered before. I hoped it wasn't a serial killer vibe I was picking up on, but knowing the kind of company my dad kept, I wouldn't be surprised.

I stepped past a group of men who were violently debating the latest scandal down at the docks and slid into the booth opposite Chaser. He raised an eyebrow and leaned forwards, resting his elbows on the table.

"Look what the cat dragged in," he drawled, giving me the once-over. His gaze lingered a little too long, and I thumped my fist onto the table.

"You need to leave me alone," I snarled.

"You can cry and beg all you like, but I'm not going anywhere."

Don't let him intimidate you, Sloane. He has to get the message; otherwise, you're gunna have to move on, leave Yvette and what little life you've managed to build behind. You're gunna have to start all over again.

"How many times do I have to say no before you get the hint?" I asked, practically seething. "Is that how you treat all women, or am I just special like that?"

He laughed and slouched back, throwing his arm over the seat again.

"You need to leave me alone or..." I began, trailing off like the lame loser I was. He knew I was all talk and my bite was duller than a butter knife.

His expression darkened. "Or *what*?"

Now he was showing his true nature. What did he do for my father? Was he a bounty hunter? A hired killer? A 'man who could get things done?' Whatever it was, it wasn't anything good. His tone suggested I didn't have any say in the matter, and one way or another, he was delivering me as promised.

When I didn't answer straight away, Chaser smirked.

It was time to leave. My expression tightened and his eyes narrowed, but I was too busy thinking about my exit strategy to dwell on it.

Choosing to leave him hanging, I slid out of the booth and left him behind, anger searing through my veins. Maybe it should've been fear, but I'd vowed to never let it get the best of me again. I had a plan and I had to follow it. Cool, calm, and collected.

When I reached the bar, I glanced at the clock.

"Yvette, I need to skip out early."

"But you still have an hour!" she exclaimed. "It's busy, Slo. You can't leave yet."

I sighed and held her shoulders so she would look at me. "Just this once. This can be your payback for all those times I've covered for you being late. Okay?"

She pouted and slouched her shoulders. "Okay. Just this once."

"Thanks," I said, letting her go. "You're a good friend, you know that?"

There wasn't much I would miss about the *Sailor's*

Arms or my anaemic paycheque-to-paycheque life, but Yvette was one of the good ones. She'd had my back.

"Can you be a doll and take the rubbish out before you leave?" she asked before I could walk away. "First and only condition."

I sighed. "Nah, yeah. Give it here."

Taking the bag, I dragged it out back and down the hall, bits of shattered glass clinking noisily as I went.

The air was cool outside, but I was alone. Music and chatter from the pub thumped behind me, and the sound of a passing siren wailed before disappearing into the distance.

Throwing the trash into the bin, the bag smacked the sides with a satisfying bang. Wiping off my hands, I turned and stumbled.

A man leaned against the wall, staring at me with a smirk on his ugly face. He was broad-shouldered, muscled, and was wearing a leather jacket, flannel shirt, and jeans. His ginger hair looked like it needed a good comb and his beard was ratty at best, but his eyes...they seemed to glow in the low light.

"Well, hello there," he drawled, his gaze raking up and down my body. "Aren't you a sight for sore eyes?"

"Entrance is 'round front," I said, taking a step back.

He smiled and pushed off the wall. Everything in my body screamed at me to run, but there was nowhere to go but back inside where Chaser was still lurking...and the door was too far away. I wouldn't make it in time.

"That's not the entrance I'm looking for." The man took a step towards me, trying to herd me into a corner.

He reached into the pocket of his leather jacket and pulled out a switchblade. Flicking it open, his lips curved into a malicious smile.

My gaze lowered and I swallowed hard. *I had to try.*

Lunging for the door, I grasped the handle, but a big hand slammed down, forcing it closed. Cool steel pressed against my throat, and I tensed.

"You can't run, little girl. Your daddy has to pay up. *Blood for blood.*"

He grabbed my hair and twisted. Pulling me away from the door, he shoved me over a crate, forcing me face down.

"Get off me!" I screeched, fighting against him.

I kicked and thrashed, but his hips held me in place. He'd thrown me down like I was nothing, and no matter how hard I struggled, I couldn't break free. Then the knife pressed against my jugular, and I whimpered, blinded by panic.

There was no way out. I was stuck. *Trapped.*

Chaser was right. There were men after me and they wouldn't stop until I was dead, but was he any better?

If I thrust my head to the side just a little, the knife would cut into an artery.

Closing my eyes, I swallowed hard.

Just a little to the side...

Do it, Sloane.

"You picked a bad night, *friend*."

The sound of Chaser's voice echoed off the brick walls, and my eyes flew open.

The knife slid against my skin, and I crumpled to the ground, my hand going to my neck. The sound of a fist slamming into flesh pulled my attention back to reality, and I gasped as the man stumbled back against the wall next to me.

Chaser shook out his hand and reached into his jacket. A second later, a knife appeared, and he held it out towards the man.

"I've got a message for you," he said. "You go back to your boss and tell him she's been claimed."

The man laughed, wiping the back of his hand across his bloodied nose. "I was wondering if I'd run into you. The infamous Chaser. *Lower than a dog.*"

Chaser's eyes narrowed, and he aimed the knife at the man's thigh and threw. The knife spun through the air and embedded into the man's flesh, almost to the hilt.

He howled in pain, and Chaser was on him in a flash, moving faster than my eyes could follow, grabbing the end of the knife and driving it all the way into the man's flesh.

"*I said,*" Chaser murmured, closing his hand around the guy's neck, "go back to your boss, and tell him if anyone comes after the girl again, I won't be so gentle. She's Fortitude property. Got it?"

"How does it feel to betray your own kind?" the man rasped.

Chaser twisted the knife, causing him to roar in pain. "Got it?"

"Okay, okay. *I've got it.*"

Ripping out the knife, Chaser shoved the man away and watched as he attempted to run. He dragged his leg behind him, disappearing into the darkness.

My hand went to my neck again, and when I pulled it back, it was red. I stared at the smear of blood, feeling sick to my stomach. It was just a nick, but I still felt lightheaded as I rose to my feet.

"Happy I stuck around?" Chaser asked, smirking at me. Always with the smirk. He smirked so much the word was losing all meaning. "Why didn't you fight? You could've taken him on your own."

I stared at him, his words barely registering. Fortitude property? A knife to my throat? *The girl has been claimed?* I had to get out of here while I still had an out. *Now.*

Backing away, I pulled the door open and darted into the pub. Weaving through the dimly lit corridor, I snatched my bag from my locker in the staff room and legged it through the bar. Glancing over my shoulder, I saw Chaser appear, his head swivelling from side to side as he searched for me.

"Hey, Bobby," I called out as I neared the door.

"Hey, Sloane," he replied, his face lighting up when he saw me. "Is everything okay?"

"See that guy over there?" I pointed Chaser out to the bouncer. "He's been giving me trouble. Can you hold him here for a while? I'm on my way home, and I don't want him to follow me."

"Sure thing, sweets."

"Thanks. You're a sweetheart." Rising to my tippy toes, he leaned down so I could kiss his cheek.

"That's what I like," he said with a chuckle. "Go on home. I'll watch out for you."

"Thanks, Bobby. See you tomorrow night." I gave him a little wave and slipped through the door, my entire body on the verge of shutting down from shock.

I couldn't stop now. I had to run.

It was time to cut ties and disappear. And this time, I'd do a better job of it.

CHAPTER 4
SLOANE

I didn't know how much time I had.

Chaser had been right about the men trying to drag me into their beef with my dad, but that didn't mean I was going anywhere with him. This wasn't a movie where the hot hero showed up and said, '*Come with me if you want to live.*' This was real life, and in it, I had to be my own hero.

Glancing over my shoulder, I hoped it was the last time I'd have to, but I knew I would be doing it for the rest of my life.

Powering through the security entrance, I ran up the stairs to the fifth floor. I had to be fast. Grab a bag and stuff in as much as I could carry.

Maybe I was doing the wrong thing or maybe I was too stupid to live, but I didn't want to choose the lesser of two evils. Death in one hand or imprisonment in the other. The smart choice would be to go for imprisonment, but that was off the table. Not when I had a chance at disappearing before I was forced into it.

I had to try.

Jogging down the hall, I rounded the corner and almost slipped and fell on my backside. A body wearing a pink robe was lying half in and half out of the doorway to an apartment, her clothing clashing with the crimson pool of blood she was lying in.

Mrs. Adelstein.

My hand flew to my mouth, and I stumbled back against the wall. The shock I'd been trying to keep at bay since that man had grabbed me out the back of the pub threatened to overwhelm me, and blood whooshed in my ears. My head spun and I struggled to draw in a breath deep enough to calm myself.

Glancing down the hall, the door to my apartment was closed, but that didn't mean anything.

Move, Sloane, I thought. *Move!*

Stepping over the pool of blood, I swallowed the vomit working its way up my throat and pulled out my keys.

I had to at least get my cash. I wasn't getting far with the twenty bucks in my pocket. I needed that money.

Raising my hand, I went to put the first key in the lock, but it never got there. A hand clamped down over my mouth, and I was pulled back against a hard chest, a strong arm trapping my arms against my sides.

I screamed and thrashed, desperate to get away. Lifting my feet off the ground, I kicked backward, aiming for anything I could.

"*Sloane*," Chaser rasped. "*Settle down.*"

Like hell. I thrashed harder, attempting to shake my head from side to side. If I could just gain enough slack, I could bite down and...

"Quiet," he murmured into my ear. "They could still be inside."

His words flipped my switch to the off-position. I slackened, and his grip loosened. When I didn't try anything, he let me go.

"Keys." He held out his hand, and I placed them into his palm.

I stood back against the wall, my knees trembling as he unlocked the door and pushed it open with the tip of his boot. It swung inwards, but nothing happened. No gunshots, no knives, no men bursting out...nothing.

I glanced down the hall. Mrs. Adelstein's hand was peeking out from her door, the pool of blood creeping farther toward the opposite wall. There was no way he could've gotten here before me.

Chaser didn't kill her.

So who did?

"Are you ready to stop running and start listening?"

"How do I know you're not one of them?" I demanded. "I have no reason to trust you."

"If I was one of them, you would've been dead long before you even saw me coming."

I tensed, my heart twisting in my chest. How long had Chaser been watching me? And more importantly, where had I slipped? I must've given myself away somewhere along the line. I had fake IDs, dealt in cash, used a scrubbed computer, and had a burner phone. I hadn't even legally changed my name or submitted any forms with my signature. I'd made up a new one to go with my new identity. *How did he know?*

"They'll be back if they aren't already on their way," he said. "Get your stuff and be quick about it."

"I'm not going with you." I fished around in my bag, looking for the present I would embed in his face.

He grabbed my arm and shook me. "Get it through your pretty little head," he said, his iridescent eyes blazing. "If you don't come with me now—"

Pressing the barrel of my gun against the side of his skull, I curled my lip. "If I don't go with you, what?"

"Put the gun down." Chaser didn't even blink; there wasn't even a twitch on his handsome face. If anything, he seemed exasperated.

"*No.*"

"We don't have time for this."

"I'm not going anywhere with you," I repeated for what felt like the umpteenth time. "So you better let me go. I'll do just fine on my own. I'm not your problem."

"You know how much of a mess firing at close

range will make?" he asked, baiting me. "You'd better close your eyes and mouth, unless you want to eat brain matter, sweetheart. Are you ready to see that? Blowing a man's head off three inches from your own face?"

The smirk faded from my lips, the gun sliding an inch down the side of his skull.

"I don't care what you think about me, and I don't care how much you hate your daddy. You're coming with me because right now, it's the only way you're walking out of here alive." Reaching up, he curled his hand around the gun, his fingers tightening on mine. "Either you pull the trigger or you get your stuff."

I didn't know when I'd begun to tremble, but I felt it the moment his icy hand covered mine. He was right; I didn't have the guts to blow his head off, just like I didn't have the guts to fight back against that guy.

I was too stupid to live and too cowardly to die.

Lowering my hand, Chaser pried the gun from my fingers, though this time, he had nothing smart to say.

"Two minutes," he said. "Two minutes, and we're gone. Okay?"

Swallowing my brewing tears, I turned and went inside and found my bag. Pulling clothes from their hangers, I shoved them into the duffel. Upending old shoeboxes full of underwear and socks, I filled in the gaps. Toiletries and makeup went next, then my textbooks and laptop. I would have to give up the bond money on this place, but uni was one thing I wasn't willing to give up on. Not yet.

Chaser stood out in the hall like he was stuck out there. He raised an eyebrow at the books but remained silent, his body angled towards the stairs.

Finally, I wedged the refrigerator away from the wall, sending a cockroach scurrying across the floor. Reaching around the back, I pulled out the resealable plastic bag filled with all the cash I had and shoved it into my handbag.

"That's it," I said. "That's all of it."

As I stepped out into the hall, Chaser's free hand bunched around the collar of my denim jacket.

Shaking him off, I hissed, "You don't need to drag me. I got the message, loud and clear."

His eyes narrowed, then he nodded. "Quickly. Follow me."

Stepping over Mrs. Adelstein's blood for the second time, we hurried down the hall and into the stairwell. Five flights down, we weren't stopped. He led me towards the back of the building, my gun still in his hand.

Chaser lingered, watching the back parking lot for a few minutes. I pressed behind him, my shoulder resting against his back. His muscles rippled as if he were reacting to me being there, but I couldn't be sure. It didn't matter, anyway.

When Chaser was satisfied no one was around, he

led me towards a car at the rear of the lot. A dark-coloured sedan with tinted windows, nothing special.

Unlocking the doors, he gestured for my duffel. Letting him take it, he threw it in the back as I got into the passenger seat.

Talk about eating my words.

Chaser got in the front and gunned the engine. The headlights switched on, illuminating the car in front as he backed out of the space before roaring out of the lot and onto the street.

Sinking back into the seat, the silence was deafening. Pressing my fingers against the cut on my neck, I checked for blood, but my finger came back clean. My pride hurt a lot more. I was supposed to be able to take care of myself...and poor Mrs. Adelstein. She was a crazy old bat, but she didn't deserve to be murdered on her doorstep.

Reality was sinking in faster than the car, which was now hurtling onto the freeway. I wasn't one to get carsick, but it was becoming a distinct possibility.

"Did he cut your neck?" Chaser asked, glancing at me. His nostrils flared and I sunk towards the window.

"Just a little."

He glanced back at the road before checking on me again. "Don't worry," he said. "I won't hurt you. I can control it."

I stared at him, my eyes widening. Control what? Was he a serial killer? Did the sight of blood excite him or something? A plan began to formulate in my mind. The first chance I got, I'd try and slip away.

Reaching into my pocket, I checked for my mobile phone. I took it out, but before I could even unlock it, Chaser snatched it from me and tossed it onto the dash. A second later, the butt of the gun smashed onto the screen, and the entire thing switched off.

"Hey!"

"You can't be Sloane anymore," he said. "Sloane is gone."

"You can't just—"

"I just did," he snapped.

"Sloane is the only person I know how to be."

He glanced at me out the corner of his eye and grunted.

"What?" I pouted.

"While you're with me, you'll do and say as you're told."

"I'm not your slave!" I exclaimed.

"It's for your own safety, *sweetheart*."

"*Don't call me that*."

"You'll do and say as you're told," he repeated, this time more firmly.

"Then?"

"Then you're your father's problem."

CHAPTER 5

CHASER

As the sun began to rise, we stopped at a rundown motel a few kilometres shy of Coolgardie.

Taking a key from the old lady behind the counter, I pushed out of the motel office and into the warmth of dawn. It was lonely country out here, the horizon flat and reddish-brown, but every time I drove across the outback on a job, it was the freest I'd ever felt.

Sloane was standing beside the car, her cheek pressed against the metal. I crossed the parking lot, and she raised her head as she heard me approach. She'd barely spoken a word for the six hours we spent on the road.

"Move," I commanded, opening the rear door and yanking out her duffel bag. Sharp corners pressed against the canvas from the inside and bashed into my leg. *How many books did she shove in there?*

"I hope you requested two singles," she said, snatching her bag off me.

"Don't worry," I drawled. "You can have the bed and the bugs all to yourself."

"What a gentleman."

Ignoring her, I popped the boot and got my stuff. Slinging the bag over my shoulder, I locked the car and went to find the room. It was only morning, but after driving all night, I figured it was best to keep our heads down for the time being. We'd get back on the road tomorrow.

Room number eight wasn't far away. Unlocking the door, I was aware of Sloane behind me. She was abrasive, rash, and all bravado, but it had me wondering if there were any teeth in it. Everything about her screamed wolf, but she hadn't fought back.

Kicking open the door, I let her go in first. She dropped her duffel onto the floor and glared at the scene before her.

The place reeked of mothballs and dampness. The whole motel had seen better days, and so had the upholstery.

All these rooms were the same, no matter where I went. Cheap floral curtains, scratchy doona covers, mould in the showers, plumbing clogged with lime and rust buildup. I'd forgotten how precious women could be about clean linen.

"This is what seventy bucks gets?" She sounded mortally wounded, and I snorted.

"Sure you don't want a cuddle?" I asked, baiting her. "We got a double."

"I'd rather die." She rolled her eyes and dragged her bag farther into the room where she flung herself onto the floor and began pulling out the contents.

I glanced over my shoulder at the empty parking lot before closing the door and turning on the light.

Sloane was illuminated by the cheap fluorescent, and for the first time, I saw her clearly. No half-light in a dingy pub, no orange streetlights, no dark corridors. I hadn't bothered looking too close outside, not when the sun was on her. One glance at her milky skin had turned my gaze right back onto the road.

We'd be back in Melbourne in a couple of days. I could do it in two, but I needed to stay sharp. Last night had shown just how close they were.

Back roads, inconspicuous motels where they didn't ask questions, and everything in cash. No planes, trains, or buses where ID was required and security cameras were on twenty-four seven. The trick was not to get into any trouble I couldn't compel our way out of.

Grimacing, I had a bad feeling trouble was already in the room.

Sitting on the end of the bed, I opened my bag and took out the gun Sloane had shoved against my head the night before. Pulling out the magazine, I checked the bullets. Narrowing my eyes, I watched her go through her clothes and smooth out the creases before refolding everything. Neat, methodical, and careful. She was taking inventory.

Sloane, or whatever she called herself now, was a runner. She'd already tried to slip away once, so I'd have to watch her like a hawk. I was forbidden to harm her, bound to my orders with blood and magic. If I touched her or delivered her with a scratch that was my fault, the boss would string me up and flay me alive.

"What the hell are you looking at?" Sloane demanded, dropping the little dress she'd had in her hands and glaring at me.

It was in that moment that I realised that she didn't know.

She didn't know what I was, what she was, or her father's true nature. How couldn't she?

Unless she hadn't turned…

That was it, wasn't it? She'd grown up away from Fortitude and when her mother died, she'd been put into the system before disappearing entirely.

She'd been attacked by a vampire and hadn't fought back. When I'd grabbed her, her strength was human, even her scent was clean.

Things had just become infinitely more complicated. Sloane didn't understand just how much danger she was in. If she knew what those vampires were capable of, she'd be singing another tune…and baying at the full moon.

"You're still staring at me," she said with a snarl.

She might not know she was a werewolf, but she had the bite of one.

"I'm having a shower," I said, ignoring her sharp tongue. "Then I'll get us some food. Don't think about leaving."

She eyed the gun in my lap, and I picked it up and slammed the magazine back into the grip. When she twigged I was taking it with me, she glanced at the car keys. Yeah, I was taking those, too.

I curled my lip as I opened the bathroom door. If Sloane didn't know, then I shouldn't tell her. Throwing a glance over my shoulder at her, she smiled sweetly.

"Don't let me keep you," she said with a pout.

Slamming the door closed, I shut her out and ran my hand over my face. Not even a day had passed, and already, I wanted to throttle her.

Turning on the shower, I undressed as steam filled the room. Seeing there was blood splattered on my T-shirt, I cursed and tossed it into the bin.

Wiping the condensation off the mirror, I stared at my reflection. *Pretty boy Chaser.*

I was many things, but to most, I was just another monster. A vampire working for wolves. Betrayer, psychopath, *inhuman.*

I'd been a part of Fortitude for the better part of a century. It was a long time on the road doing what I did. Hunting down the scum of the earth, settling scores, working the other side. I was the nameless ghost who walked in, solved problems with blood and violence, and walked out golden...all in the name of the Fortitude Wolves, the alpha pack of the East Coast.

There was a reason they called me Chaser. I chased blood and money, and nothing else.

I was the guy in the corner you didn't mess with. I was the guy who didn't blink when I took the shot. I was the guy who didn't care about how many people I'd killed. I was the guy who worked best alone. I was the guy who the boss 'trusted' to get his little girl...who wasn't so little anymore.

All I cared about was the job. *All I cared about was the job.*

When I finally emerged from the bathroom, Sloane was still on the floor where I'd left her...oblivious to the dark world of werewolves and vampires.

CHAPTER 6

SLOANE

I should've made a break for it, but I didn't know where the hell we were. Outside, there was nothing but trees and road. Even I knew running blindly into the outback with no water or map was a death sentence.

And it wasn't until Chaser had turned on the shower that I realised he'd stolen my money *and* my fake ID. He was a real piece of work, that one.

I had zero illusions that this was one of those fun cross-country road trips. I was cargo; I wouldn't have any say on how or where. The only thing I was good for was sitting still and keeping my mouth shut.

Despite the eventful night, I wasn't tired. I figured it had something to do with the adrenaline or the shock, maybe both. My mind raced, my thoughts full of images of the man out the back of the pub, Chaser shoving him off me like he weighed nothing, and poor Mrs. Adelstein dead in the hallway.

Yvette must be worried about me. When I don't show tonight, she'll beg the boss to check the security footage. Then they'd see the moment that man attacked me out back. Then the cops would link it to the murder at the apartments, giving me an alibi, but putting me and my fake identity on their radar.

Rolling my eyes at the shadowed roof, I studied the rise and fall of the popcorn ceiling. I knew the last thing the pub owners would want was police sniffing around—especially not when there was a borderline illegal trade happening out the side door. They thought the staff didn't see the money fly under the table, but we did. Like any of it mattered anymore.

No one was coming for me. At least, no one good.

Rolling over, I squinted, trying to make out Chaser's features in the dark. He'd taken the spare blankets and pillows out of the closet and made a makeshift bed on the floor. I'd complained until I was blue in the face, but he'd still closed every curtain against the sun and forced me to sleep.

His chest rose and fell, the gun lying on top of his sternum, his right hand curled around the grip. At this angle, he didn't look like the hard biker bounty hunter I assumed he was. He looked like...a boy. Nothing but a boy with a toy gun.

Sighing, I rolled over onto my other side. I was stuck

for the moment—until I could nick my money back off him—but it wasn't that bad, was it? He hadn't tried to lay his hands on me, and he'd saved me from that man.

Maybe I could convince him to take me some place else, far away from my father. *Maybe...*

I must have finally fallen asleep because I remembered seeing a full moon. I'd dreamt about them often enough that I'd become immune to the image, putting it down to a silly little quirk in my subconscious.

This time it burned a dull burnished gold, rearing over the horizon as the sun set. It was abnormal, how it hung amongst the fiery glow, and it dominated my line of sight. I could see the dark splotches of ancient craters and trace the rise and fall of the destruction with my gaze.

I'd raised my hand, reaching towards it, wanting to touch—

"Sloane."

My eyes cracked open, and I moaned. Chaser was standing over me, backlit by the window, which was full of the orange blaze of sunset. It felt like I'd only just fallen asleep.

"Get up," he barked, pulling the doona off me.

"Hey!" I scrambled, trying to yank it back up.

Luckily, I'd slept in a T-shirt long enough to cover my assets, so there wasn't much for him to see.

"You've got ten minutes. I want you ready by the time I get back from the office."

Before I could open my mouth, he strode from the room and slammed the door closed behind him. A few doors down, a dog barked.

Snatching the clothes I'd laid out that morning, I darted into the shower and had a quick scrub. If I wasn't out and dressed in ten, there was no doubt in my mind Chaser would be in here, dragging me out by the hair...even if I was naked and covered in soap suds.

I dressed in a pair of black skinny jeans, a beat-up black T-shirt, my faded denim jacket with the ripped pockets, and boots. Glancing in the mirror, I fluffed up my hair and pouted. Glancing at the little pouch of makeup, I rolled my eyes. *What was the point?*

Chaser wasn't back when I emerged from the bathroom, so I grabbed my bag and went outside. Standing by the car, I surveyed the parking lot and the highway beyond.

There was nothing but cracked asphalt and patchy greenish-grey scrub as far as the eye could see. A road train—a semi hauling three trailers—rumbled past, lit up like a carnival ride.

The indicators on the car flashed orange, and the locks clicked as they disengaged. Glancing around, I saw Chaser through the window of the office, chatting up some old lady. Wrenching the door open, I slipped into the front passenger seat.

Opening the glove compartment, I rifled through

the contents, but I found nothing useful, not even a spare pair of sunglasses.

The driver's side door opened, and Chaser got in.

"Looking for something?" he asked.

"I was looking for something to bash your skull in with," I retorted.

"Good luck with that." He put the key into the ignition and turned the engine on. Throwing his arm back, he curled his hand around the corner of my seat and looked over his shoulder as he backed out of the parking space.

He turned onto the highway and gunned it.

"Put your seat belt on," he ordered, reaching over me and tugging at the belt.

Slapping his arm away, I wrenched the seat belt across my body and clipped it in place. "Happy?"

"Far from it."

Glaring at him, I studied the side of his face, searching for a flicker of something I could manipulate, but all I found was hostility.

"What are you looking at?" he snapped.

"So, if you work for my father, you're in his gang of losers," I declared. "You don't look like a biker."

"Looks can be deceiving. How old are you?"

"Why do you want to know?"

He narrowed his eyes and turned back to the road. "You're twenty-five."

"Why'd you bother asking if you already knew?" I snorted and kicked my feet up onto the dash.

"Get your feet down," he snapped, shoving my boots.

"Where's your bike, huh? And your leathers? Since when do bikers ferry around cargo in a Toyota Camry?"

"I know you're trying to bait me," he said, not taking his eyes off the road. "It won't work, so do yourself a favour and keep quiet."

"So?"

"So what?"

"Where's your bike?"

He glanced at me from out the corner of his eye but didn't reply.

"Do you even know what *fortitude* means?" I went on.

"Courage in pain and adversity," he deadpanned.

"Are you really that brainwashed?" I asked, curling my lip. "You're spouting off the company motto like it's a religion."

"What I think is irrelevant."

I stared at him, measuring his abrasive coldness. His movements were precise, like he was on autopilot. Like he'd done this many times before. He did what he was told and never deviated from his orders.

"You believe in it all, don't you?" I asked. "The motto, the brotherhood, the criminal activity. You don't care who you hurt."

Chaser's hands tightened around the steering wheel. "Shut up, Sloane."

"You don't care if you hurt me."

"How I wish I could compel you to shut up," he muttered, focusing on the road ahead.

"Violence, crime, pain, suffering... You want to take me back to that? My mother spent her entire life trying to keep me away from it until she died. I don't want any part of it. I don't care who's trying to kill me. *I want to disappear.*"

"I said shut up," Chaser hissed.

"What kind of future do you think I'll have if you take me back there?" I snarled, anger welling up so fiercely, I almost felt like snatching the wheel and running us off the road.

"I will throw you in the boot if you keep testing me, Sloane."

"What do you get out of it? Money? Power? Drugs?"

Everyone and everything in life had an ulterior motive. It was called personal gain. No one cared about other people's feelings. Even love was a sham. My mum loved my dad enough to make me, and even though she got out, it still got her killed. That was how much it mattered.

"You keep talking, but I don't answer," he drawled, not looking at me. "You're living up to the definition of insanity, Sloane."

I curled my hand around the seat belt and scowled. Chaser was saving me from a terrible fate, but he was delivering me to one just as shitty. He wasn't turning around or letting me go. He was a sheep who would follow orders or die trying. I'd tried to bait him and win him to my side, but at least now I knew who's side he was truly on. Spoiler alert...*it wasn't mine.*

It just goes to show that you can never trust a pretty face.

Sighing, I turned towards the window and stared at the passing landscape. It was time to formulate an escape plan. There were still a few thousand kilometres from here to Melbourne.

"What? Giving up so soon?" Chaser asked.

"You love the fight, Chaser," I retorted, "and the things you love...? I would rather die than give them to you."

CHAPTER 7
SLOANE

With all hopes for a *Thelma and Louise*-style road trip dashed, all I could do was sit and wait.

Watching the landscape change outside the car window, I studied the horizon. A bluish-purple tinge faded upwards with a smear of clouds that broke it all up into pieces. Night was upon us, the last of the day fading into a blanket of star-studded indigo.

Trees flanked either side of the road. Then a yellow road sign flashed past, reflecting in the headlights, warning drivers of crossing wildlife. Farther along, a hand-painted placard advertising food and fuel loomed out of the shadows, telling us it was only two kilometres to the next roadhouse.

Chaser turned the car off the highway and onto a smaller piece of asphalt that led towards the roadhouse.

My stomach squirmed, hoping for something edible and a way out of this mess. Pressing my nose against the window, my hopes were dashed when I saw the population count on the welcome sign. *Three.*

So, the plan remained the same for now. Play along, give Chaser what he wanted, fish for information on who was after my dad, and the moment his guard slipped, I'd make a break for it. As long as the break was in a populated area with adequate means of transportation and evasion—from both parties.

The roadhouse wasn't much to look at. It was a 'blink and you'll miss it' kind of set up. The garage had two pumps and a sign displaying the current per litre price. It looked like it'd been originally built sometime in the '70s and had various, so-called 'modern upgrades' tacked on here and there to modernise it.

When he cut the engine, Chaser flung the door open and got out.

Following his lead, I slid out of the tin can and rounded the bonnet, stretching my arms over my head. Man, my backside was numb.

A few 4WDs with caravans hitched on the back were parked near the pub, and one lonely truck and trailer, but we were the only people at the bowsers.

Chaser eyed me, the muscles in his bare arms tensing.

Resigning myself to the fact there was no chance of escape without causing a scene, I leaned against the side of the car. Squinting my eyes in the half-light, I watched the display tick over dollars and litres as he filled the tank.

"What's he into this time?" I asked, fishing for information.

Chaser grunted.

"Dad?" I prodded. "Has he graduated from petty turf wars fought with Molotov cocktails?"

"He can explain that," he replied. "It's not my business."

"If you're Fortitude, then it is your business."

"Maybe you misheard me. It's not my business *to tell you*."

"It must be something heavy," I went on after a moment. "Full-on mafia. Has to be if some guy is trying to attack me on the other side of the country. Especially since I'm not part of his family."

He shook his head and his jaw tensed. "You really don't know, do you?"

"I know enough." I kicked the toe of my boot against the side of the pump.

He raised an eyebrow and pulled the nozzle out of the fuel tank. "I thought you'd cry more."

"Excuse me?" I scoffed. "Just because I'm a woman, doesn't mean—"

Chaser grunted and curled his lip. "That's not what I meant."

"This world is already screwed up," I told him. "Either that, or I've seen too many violent movies and been desensitised to it, even when it's happening to me."

"That's not a good thing." He returned the nozzle to the pump.

"*Duh.*"

"I'm going inside. Get back in the car."

Shoving off the side of the car, I darted between the pumps and sauntered towards the automatic doors. Chaser was beside me in an instant.

"I said—"

"Get over yourself. I'm not going to do a runner."

He grabbed my arm and pulled me to his side, making me stumble.

"*I'm hungry,*" I declared, tensing at his closeness. His fingers felt like unbreakable steel closing around my flesh.

"Get back in the car, and I'll bring you something."

His attitude was really wearing me down.

"Chaser, we're in the middle of nowhere." I waved my hands around, forcing him to let me go. "Who's going to find us out here? And more importantly, where am I going to run to? Believe me, I've already done the math."

He scowled at me but I stood my ground, glaring right back. Our staring competition went on for a full minute before he cracked.

"If you squeal, there'll be trouble," he told me.

"Give me some credit." I flicked my hair over my

shoulder. "I'm a survivor, Chaser, and right now, you're my best chance."

He rolled his eyes. "Get inside before I change my mind."

The automatic doors swished open as we approached, which was quite the technological feat for an out-of-the-way roadhouse.

Inside, it seemed to double as the local store. There were shelves of everyday groceries, along with cheap hardware and a rack of magazines. Lingering by the chocolates, I eyed a Mars bar as Chaser paid for the petrol. They were yapping about the weather when a stand of sunglasses caught my eye.

Turning it around, I perused the selection while studying Chaser in the mirror. After crossing the Nullarbor, there was a border checkpoint where they canvassed for fruit and vegetables. I'd never realised it was a thing until I'd moved across country, but biosecurity was a serious thing between states. There might be someone there who could help get me away from Chaser, even though it was still an isolated place. But still, it was the only border crossing for hundreds of kilometres.

Picking up a pair of aviator sunglasses with a blue tint on the lenses, I slipped them on. Angling my head from side to side, I studied my reflection and concluded that I looked badarse.

"Hey," I said, calling out to Chaser, who was still at the counter. "Give me five bucks."

He turned and glared while the attendant—a man who seemed to be in his thirties—looked at me with interest.

"Why?" Chaser asked.

"I want these." I turned my head from side to side so he could see. "How do I look?"

"Put those back," he barked.

"You look good," the guy behind the counter said.

"See?" I pointed at the guy and pouted at Chaser. "Five bucks won't emasculate you."

Chaser rolled his eyes and handed a note to the attendant. "The petrol and the sunglasses."

The cash register dinged as the money exchanged hands, and I admired myself in the mirror once more for good measure. A moment later, I was dragged outside and towards the pub.

"Hey!"

Ignoring my protests, Chaser towed me across the yard, through another door, and into the pub. He strode up to the woman behind the bar, letting me follow behind.

"What can I get you?" she asked, leaning forwards and placing her hand on the bar.

"A hamburger with the lot, with chips and tomato sauce on the side," I rattled off my order. "And a Coke. *A big one.*"

The woman raised an eyebrow at Chaser. "And you?"

"Double it," he said, not taking his eyes off me. He

handed her a yellow fifty-dollar note. "Keep the change."

"Right," she said taking the money. "Sit anywhere you like. I'll bring your food over when it's ready."

Chaser's gaze was making me uncomfortable, and I watched the woman shout our order to the cook.

He grabbed my wrist and dragged me along a row of tables before practically shoving me into a seat by the window. He sat opposite, his expression pure thunder.

A table full of grey nomads—over-fifty-fives who travelled around in their caravans long-term—were eyeing us but didn't try to butt in.

"Careful with that grip of yours, people are watching," I murmured.

Chaser snorted and leaned back, drawing my attention away from the oldies and back to him.

"You know, you really need to lay off with the manhandling," I told him. "It's giving people the wrong impression."

He ground his teeth, signalling he was about to blow a gasket.

"You run with bikers, but I don't think you're one. Not really," I added, reaching for a serviette, which I laid over my lap.

He glanced out the window. "That's a dangerous observation."

"Avoiding eye contact…" I mused. "*Interesting.*"

"You're the biggest pain in the arse I've ever met,"

he said with a snarl, leaning over the table. "You're childish, petulant, and borderline stupid."

"Petulant? That's a big word for a tricycle tyrant." I smiled sweetly even though his words cut.

He was right about all of it. It was beyond time to grow up, and I'd done that the moment I'd left the foster system all those years ago. But ever since Chaser showed up... Riling him up was the best entertainment going around, and I wasn't going to make things easy for him. By the time I found a window of opportunity, he'd be begging to get rid of me. Win-win.

"The problem is," he went on, my insult bouncing off his hard outer shell, "all that nonsense coming out of your mouth is bravado. That's not who you are."

I tensed. "How would you know?"

"Professional experience."

The sunglasses felt heavy on top of my head. Just when I thought I had him pegged, he said something that threw me off course. He didn't look like a biker, but it didn't mean he was or wasn't. He could've come from anywhere.

"I guess we've both got things to hide," he said, studying me.

"So you don't deny it."

"You'd be a moron to believe people weren't lying to you about something. Even when they say they're being transparent."

"Humanity sucks," I said.

He licked his lips. "It has its uses."

"I've never met a single person I would die for."

He laughed like I'd just told the funniest joke ever and ran his hand over his face.

"What?" I demanded, giving him the dirtiest look I could muster.

"You're really self-centred. I'll have to add that to the list."

My mouth fell open. "Excuse me?"

"Wake up, princess," he said, his lip curling. "Most people haven't found the one. I would go as far to say that that kind of thing happens to one in a trillion, and there ain't a trillion people on this pathetic excuse of a rock. You need to readjust your expectations."

"And where should I readjust them to? My father? *You?*"

He shrugged, falling silent as the woman dumped our order onto the table.

"Enjoy," she drawled, slamming the two Cokes down so violently, some of the soft drink sloshed onto the table.

"I think *she* needs to readjust her expectations," I said the moment she walked away.

"You can never trust someone completely, Sloane," Chaser said. "That's just facts."

I made a face. "Oh, you're preaching to the choir."

"The only thing you need to believe about me is that I won't let you die. Whatever else you think doesn't matter."

I stared at him, the smell of the cooked food

making my stomach growl. His head tilted slightly to the side, signalling he was waiting. For what, who knew?

He wouldn't let me die? I wasn't sure if I should flip him the bird or throw him a parade. This push and pull we had going on was wearing thin. One second he wasn't so bad, but then he shoved everything away with his stellar personality. He was real top-shelf material.

"If you're waiting for some kind of epiphany from me, you're not getting one," I said. Picking up my burger, I took a bite that sent sauce up my face and lettuce hanging out my mouth. "*Bon appétit.*"

CHAPTER 8

CHASER

I refused to believe Sloane was that childish. She was the daughter of an alpha.

She was putting together an escape plan, that much was clear. Annoy the hell out of me, steal her stuff back, then leg it into a crowd, hoping I'd be glad to see the back of her.

That's how my targets usually did it, but I always found them. After that, things usually became worse... for them, not me.

Don't disappoint me, Chaser. You know what happens when you do.

I squeezed my eyes shut. One shot was all it took to destroy someone's life. One shot to bind them to you forever.

Death begat death, and revenge begat revenge. Round and round it went, and it never stopped.

In the end, it wasn't worth it. It fixed nothing.

It didn't bring her back, and now I was stuck, and it wasn't just in another motel room with yet another descendant of the wolf who'd tricked me into flushing my life down the toilet... Endless servitude caused by a debt that would never be repaid—a life for a life.

Hindsight was brutal, especially for the immortal.

I let the shower run as I ate, gulping down the bag of blood I'd smuggled inside, still in two minds on whether I should break the supernatural news to Sloane or not.

Tomorrow we'd hit the vast expanse of nothing called the Nullarbor Plain—the straightest stretch of road in Australia at 145.6 km. There'd be little in the way of food between here and the Western Australian border, and I had no time or desire to go chasing animals across the outback. I could forget about carrying blood bags in the dry heat, too.

I had to gorge myself and hope I didn't get high.

When I was done, I turned off the shower and opened the door.

Sloane was laying on the bed, in the top she liked to sleep in, reading a book that looked more like a brick than anything else. I narrowed my eyes at the sight before me—my vision sharper now that I'd fed—and closed the door with a bang.

She didn't flinch.

Rubbing my damp hair with a threadbare towel, I tossed it over the back of a chair.

"What's that?" I asked, unable to hold on to my curiosity.

"It's a book," she retorted. "You know, with the pages and the words and the stuff."

"Hilarious."

Stepping past her, I grabbed the book and tore it from her grasp. She kicked up a stink as I turned it over in my hands.

"*Theory and Methods in Political Science,*" I read aloud. "What's this for?"

"I'm working on a university degree," she said, snatching the book back. "I'm not giving up on it just because you kidnapped me."

"I wouldn't call it kidnapping," I said, the word 'university' the last thing I was expecting her to say. It was another clue to the interior she was hiding underneath all that childishness.

"You're forcing me to go with you against my will. That's kidnapping."

Snorting, I glanced at the bright yellow highlighter in her hand.

"What do you want that book for anyway?" I went on. "You want to be a politician?"

She shrugged.

"You've got the mouth for it." I tossed the book onto the bed.

"I don't know what I want to be," she said, rolling

her eyes. "But I don't want to be dumb doing whatever it is. Knowledge is power."

I raised an eyebrow, my gaze dropping to the book again. That was a mystery I wasn't sure I wanted to unravel.

Leaving her to her studies, or whatever she wanted to call it, I sat at the table and turned on the television. I scrolled through the channels, looking for a local news station, but I couldn't help glancing at her again.

Her head was buried in her book, the highlighter squeaking across the page.

She didn't trust or believe other people had her best interests at heart, but here she was, still trying to invest in her future with that stupid book. And I was taking her back to a life that could only end in tragedy, even though she was on a hit list.

I was stuck, and now, so was she.

I could say I didn't care all I wanted, but I didn't have a choice. Orders were orders.

She was a Marini Wolf...and one in a million. Her life was never going to be her own.

CHAPTER 9
SLOANE

Turning off the shower, I dried myself off, patting the threadbare towel over my body.

That morning, I'd woken up on the side of the bed labeled 'frustrated.' The longer Chaser and I were on this screwed-up road trip to hell, the more confused I became. It was like I'd stepped into some parallel universe where nothing was as it seemed.

I was beginning to doubt that the bad guys Chaser had decided he was there to protect me from even existed. If it weren't for the very real encounter with that guy behind the *Sailor's Arms*, and the pool of blood Mrs. Adelstein had been lying in, I would've laughed in his face.

I studied myself in the mirror as I towel-dried my hair. I'd never put much thought into my looks before. I was just a plain girl keeping her head down. I wasn't exactly ugly, but I never put in much effort.

My hair wasn't coloured, I didn't get my nails done, and I had no idea what my eyebrows were doing. I knew people plucked them, or waxed, or *something*... but I'd never put much brain power into thinking about it.

I guessed I saw myself as average. My gaze lowered, taking in the rest of my body. I guess I wasn't overweight or anything... *Bloody hell, Sloane. Why do you care?*

Rolling my eyes, I pulled on my clothes. Sitting on the closed toilet lid, I towelled my hair once more and tossed it onto the floor, my gaze catching on something hidden in the bin.

A wad of toilet paper had been stuffed inside, which was nothing special, but it was stained with dark splotches of reddish brown that looked an awful lot like blood.

Curiosity got the better of me and I lifted the wad of paper with the tip of my pinky finger. A heavy-duty plastic bag was wrapped up inside, full of something red. Blood, I realised. It *was* blood.

Pulling back a bit more of the paper, I realised it was one of those hospital baggies—the kind they kept blood inside with all those tubes to hook up to IVs and other fancy machines.

I curled my nose and let the paper fall back into place. What was Chaser doing with it? Did he have some kind of secret illness? Was it a drug thing? Maybe the room hadn't been entirely cleaned between guests

and I was reading too much into it. If it wasn't Chaser's,
then *gross*.

Then again, I was dealing with Fortitude and my
father. It could be absolutely anything. I'd have to keep
my mind sharp and my eyes peeled.

Time to level up, Sloane.

I washed my hands in case it was a biohazard-type
deal and pushed out of the bathroom. I sat on the end
of the bed, but Chaser didn't even look at me. The
moment the bathroom was free, he strode into it and
slammed the door behind him.

Maybe I *was* reading too much into it.

Picking up my textbook, I shoved it into my bag. It
was nearly impossible to study while Chaser stared at
me like I'd sprouted a second head. Did he think it was
a waste of time to get a degree? *Pfft*, what would he
know? It was a miracle he even knew what a book was.

Looking at his bag, I felt the telltale signs of
temptation. My money might be in there. Glancing at
the bathroom door, my mind went blank as I realised
the door hadn't closed. A gap the width of my palm
granted me access to the ultimate peep show, and
another kind of temptation reared its ugly head.

Gross. I made a face and turned away.

What *was* that blood bag for? I shook my head and
pulled on my boots. Like I could ask him. I'd done
enough to rile the guy up and asking if he had a secret
illness was a step too far...which was saying something
considering the mouth I had.

When Chaser emerged from the bathroom, I dragged my bag out to the car while he returned the room key.

Waiting for my chauffeur in the front seat of the car, I watched as he appeared around the corner and strode towards me. Broad shoulders, his T-shirt clung to his muscled chest, the edges of his tattoo peeking out of the collar, his stubbled jaw, and hair that fell forwards over his brow. He looked like an ordinary tough guy—just another criminal in a long line waiting back in Melbourne. He didn't look sick *or* high. If I had to choose between the two, I'd guess he was hiding a secret tumour, providing the blood bag was his. Maybe I should check for track marks…

When Chaser got in the car, he shoved my feet off the dashboard. "How many times do I have to tell you to keep your feet down?"

Putting on my five-dollar sunglasses, I made a face. My gaze lowered, studying every inch of him. He was wearing a jacket, but maybe there was a prick or two on the back of his hand. He was well-aware I was staring because his hand tightened on the gear stick.

I'd noticed he had a sloppy way of driving. He leaned slightly to the side while his right hand sat on the steering wheel and his left lay either on his lap or on the centre console. Today, I noticed he had a smear of black ink on his right thumb between the joints.

"What's this?" I grasped his hand and lifted it so I could see the tattoo on his thumb. His skin was cold, like there was no warmth inside him—matched his personality.

"It's my stamp of approval," he replied dryly.

It was a tattoo that looked like a crude rendering of two crossed swords. I knew that image—the Fortitude logo—and it made me want to puke. Yeah, Fortitude had a logo like they were some kind of corporate conglomeration with a business card.

"They mark you now?" I demanded.

"It's just a tattoo."

"It's not just a tattoo. It's a brand."

"Why do you care? All you've been doing since I met you is push my buttons." He snatched his hand back and glared, his thundercloud personality raining all over the place. "You've really gotta stop."

"Get over yourself," I hissed. I pushed my sunglasses back up my nose and sank back into the seat. "God forbid someone might actually *care*."

"You? Care about me?" he scoffed, turning over the engine.

"Is it such a foreign concept?"

"With the way you've been acting since I picked you up...? Yeah, it is."

"It's nothing personal."

"That's not going to change my mind."

"Do you want me to change your mind?" I asked, my voice low.

"*Sloane*." His tone had softened considerably.

"*Chaser*."

He grunted and peeled out of the parking space, and the moment we hit the highway, he flattened his foot on the accelerator. The car shot forwards, the engine revving as it flicked through the gears.

Sitting there, trapped in the passenger seat, was the first time I really looked at Chaser. I meant, *really looked* at him beyond his rough exterior.

Other than the first night we'd spent together, he'd made sure I got the first shower, the first meal, and I got the bed while he slept on either the floor or in a chair. He tensed every time I stared at him for too long, and he bit my head off whenever my words got too close for comfort.

Was Chaser finally cracking? Did I want him to? After seeing that blood bag, I wasn't quite sure *what* I was dealing with.

"I need to go to the toilet," I declared, mainly wanting to get away from him for a few blessed minutes. My bladder was perfectly fine.

"We just left the bloody motel," he snapped. "*Hold it.*"

"I'm not going to pee in the middle of the Nullarbor."

Ten minutes of uneasy silence went by, and finally, Chaser turned off the road, and we came to an abrupt halt beside a petrol bowser at a lonely BP servo. The lot beside us was empty, as was the highway behind us, until a lone truck rumbled by, but after that, we were alone again.

Following the sign painted on the side of the building, I cursed when I realised the door to the restroom was locked. A sign riveted onto the brick wall said *Key for Paying Customers Only.*

Storming inside, I asked the attendant for the key and pointed to Chaser, who paced outside. "He's paying for some petrol once he's done wearing a hole in the concrete."

"Well..." the man eyed me before he reluctantly handed me the key, "all right."

Glancing through the window, I saw Chaser's back was turned. He was scanning the road, watching cars swish past. Looking at the key in my hand, I knew this was my chance. I might have five, maybe six minutes before he came looking. If I was going, it had to be now.

Pushing out the side door, I saw the sign hanging over the toilet. My boots crunched on gravel and the key felt like it weighed a million tonnes.

All I had to do was climb the chain-link fence, cross the empty lot, and disappear into the ravine. A short climb up the other side and I would lose him on the road back into town. There was enough traffic headed back west that I could flag someone down.

I hesitated. Why was I so confused? His stellar personality hadn't put this much doubt into me.

A gunshot rang out across the open lot and the wall splintered beside my head. Letting out a scream, I dropped to my knees and scurried behind the brick fence separating the side door from the open space beyond.

I flung my arms over my head and my heart jack hammered when I heard boots thunder towards me.

"She's there!" an unfamiliar voice shouted.

Glancing up, I caught sight of Chaser peering around the corner, and my eyes widened.

He raised his finger to his lips. Then he raised his hand, revealing a gun plastered in it.

He fired once, the boom echoing across the open space, and a split-second later, a man grunted in pain. It was this loud *oomph* on the other side of the wall that made me almost crap my pants. *He'd been so close.*

"Chaser…" I cried, not knowing which way to run.

"Stay down." He was a handful of steps away from me, but it felt like a million miles. Rounding the corner, he moved towards me, the gun held high.

I was such a mess. I thought I could run from Chaser and take care of myself? *Fat chance.* I'd turned to water the moment that bullet zoomed past my face. I was a coward, a little girl waiting for a man to save her.

Grasping my hand, Chaser pulled me behind the wall and into the open. We took one step, and movement flashed as a man leaped out from behind the old sign where he'd been taking cover. He raised his gun and fired. Just like that, no hesitation.

Chaser reacted instantly. He shoved me to the side, and I fell, my knees hitting the ground as the bullet flew past. He fired back. *Pop, pop, pop.*

"*Sloane.*" Chaser held out his hand and I gasped. Blood was trickling down his arm, covering his palm and fingers.

"You're bleeding."

"Get up. We have to go. *Now.*"

"Where's the other guy?"

"Dead." He nodded across the yard where a man was crumpled against the chain-link fence. "*Do you get it now?*"

"*I get it!*" I exclaimed. "Okay? *I get it.*"

Scrambling to my feet, I felt like throwing up, but I followed Chaser to the car, aware of the dull sound of approaching sirens. It'd been self-defence, but Chaser had still opened fire and killed two men. Suddenly, the thought of him being locked up sent a wave of nausea through me.

That was when he stumbled and bashed against the car, leaving a smear of blood on the window.

Chaser had been shot.

He'd pushed me out of the way and had taken a bullet meant for me.

"Give me the keys," I demanded, springing into action.

"Leave it," he barked.

"You've been shot and if you can't hear that, those are sirens. Now give me the keys!"

Hissing, he tossed them at me, and I caught them against my chest. Rushing around the bonnet, I got into the driver's seat and shoved the key into the ignition. I turned the engine over the moment Chaser shut the passenger side door.

The car roared into life, and I manoeuvred us through the pumps and towards the road. Fishtailing out onto the highway, I slammed my foot on the accelerator, and the car jolted forwards, tyres squealing before propelling us away from the servo.

Chaser grasped his arm, tearing away the torn material of his jacket so he could check the damage.

"What now?" I asked, my hands—and practically everything else—shaking. "How bad is it? Do we need to go to a hospital?"

"No. No hospitals," he hissed as he poked and prodded at his arm.

"But what if—"

"*They can't help me.*"

As he shucked off his jacket and tore strips out of the lining, I loosened my grip on the wheel and focused on the road ahead. When he grunted in obvious pain, I glanced back and saw he'd tied a tourniquet just above his bicep.

"Where do we go from here?" I asked, checking the mirrors, thankful the road was empty behind us. On the edge of the outback, there was nowhere to go but back the way we came or down to the coast. Going forwards wasn't an option.

"South," Chaser said, settling back into the seat. "Go south."

CHAPTER 10

SLOANE

I drove with no destination for a long time.

The sun was on our right, which meant it was mid-afternoon. Without a watch, I was flying olden-days style. You know, navigation by celestial bodies and all that shit...and road signs. Ahead, a green slab of metal told me it was ten kilometres to Esperance.

Chaser had said nothing since we left the BP. He hadn't lost consciousness or kicked the bucket; he'd just not said a single word. It wasn't reassuring considering the amount of blood he'd lost and the lack of direction he'd given other than south. So I just drove with one eye on the road ahead and one behind.

The fact we weren't being followed meant nothing. It was only a matter of time before someone caught up with us. That's what worried me the most. We were still on the west side of the country, and there were a lot of kilometres, cops, and bad guys between Melbourne and us. *A lot.*

After a while, Chaser reached up and untied the tourniquet around his upper arm. Slowly at first, then he untied it entirely and tossed it onto the floor.

I eyed him, trying to see if more red stuff was pouring from his arm.

"Has the bleeding stopped?" I asked after a moment.

"Yeah."

"That's good, right?"

"For now." He narrowed his eyes, giving me a suspicious once-over.

"What does that mean?"

"It means I need to look at it when we stop." He glanced out the window. "Where are we?"

"Esperance."

"Esperance?" he groaned.

"You said south, so I went south," I shot back. "There isn't anywhere else to go out here, Chaser. There's only one road."

The city limits loomed in the distance. Streetlights turned on as the sky darkened, and I saw a sign for a motel coming up on the left. The thought of having to sleep in the car wasn't appealing in the slightest.

"I'm pulling in," I declared, veering off the road.

Chaser didn't argue, which was a boost to my confidence. This must've been the first smart thing I'd done since this chaos began.

Stopping the car by the main office, I turned off the engine and held out my hand.

"Give me some money," I demanded.

Chaser grunted and went to get out of the car, but I reached over him and jerked the door closed.

"You're not going into that office with blood all over you," I said.

"It's fine."

"No, it's not. Blood means questions, and we don't need any of those right now." Straightening up, I cupped his cheek and forced his face towards mine. "For once in your life, *trust me.*"

For a split-second, I thought I felt him open up a little, but he jerked away. Reaching into his back pocket with his good hand, he presented me with a fistful of notes.

Snatching the cash from him, I slipped out of the car before he changed his mind.

I got us a room at the back of the motel, convincing the lady at the reception desk we preferred not to deal with the road noise. Eighty bucks with a twenty change later, I got back into the car and drove us around to the rear. I found a spot by the door to our room, and luckily for us, it was away from any prying eyes. A blood-soaked man was exactly the thing people called triple zero to anonymously tip about.

The room wasn't much to look at, but they never were—not in recent experience, anyway. There was a double bed, a table and chairs, a sink with a kettle and microwave, a TV, and a separate bathroom. Ironically, even with the awful mustard-colour scheme, it was larger and way more furnished than my studio apartment.

Chaser sat at the table and checked his arm. In the disgusting lighting, he looked really sick. Now that I had time to study it, I realised the bullet had grazed his arm to the point it had carved his flesh apart, straight across the surface like a stone skipping over water.

"Do you need a Band-Aid?" I asked, not knowing if he needed stitches or something sticky to keep the cut together.

"There's a first-aid kit in the boot of the car."

"I don't think that's—"

"*Sloane.*" He glared at me and pointed toward the door.

I held up my hands. "Fine."

Reaching for the keys, I stumbled as his hand caught my wrist. He gave me a pointed look that had everything to do with this being a test, and I shook him off.

Stalking outside, I popped the boot and fished around in the half-light. My duffel was there, and so was his.

A familiar feeling of temptation reared its ugly head.

I could jump in the car and vanish. It would be

easy with Chaser inside and me out here with the keys. I'd been planning on dumping him that morning. I could still do it...

I hesitated.

But...

Maybe...

I glanced at the door to the motel room.

The only thing that stopped me was the dull ringing in my ears from the gunshots and my aching knees. Sighing, I grabbed the first-aid kit and slammed the boot closed.

Going back into the motel room, I made sure the door was locked behind me. I dumped the kit onto the table, eyeing a shirtless and bloody Chaser.

He wasn't... Ugh, I wasn't sure I wanted to see this.

Still, I couldn't look away as he took the kit and opened it.

"Do you want any help with that?" I asked, edging around the table and sitting beside him.

"No."

He picked up a pair of tweezers, and without even blinking, shoved the tip inside his torn flesh and began pulling something out of the path the bullet had carved across his upper arm.

My eyes widened as he wiped bloodied splinters on the towel. "What *is* that?"

"Wood." He shoved the tweets back in and began digging into his torn flesh.

He'd been shot with wooden bullets. Why would someone want to shoot at us with wooden bullets?

Staring at his chest and torso, I could now see several other scars. Pink, puckered lines that'd been sewn together by someone who had zero finesse. My mind went back to the gunfight at the service station, and I realised something important about him. He knew how to shoot. It wasn't just the simple point and fire kind of bullshit. No, he knew *how to shoot to kill.*

"Who are you?" I whispered, my stomach rolling.

Ignoring me, he continued to work until he was satisfied that he'd found all the splinters. Then he wiped the blood off his skin with a piece of cloth from the kit.

Without a word, I reached over and cleaned up the mess on the table. A blood bag, wooden bullets… things were getting weird.

"Sloane."

"What?" I picked up the tweezers and wiped them off before putting them back inside the first-aid kit.

"I dropped the ball today."

Freezing, I looked up, our gazes meeting. Something had changed. Something I couldn't quite put my finger on.

"It doesn't matter," I murmured. "We got out of it."

"We shouldn't have been in it at all." His eyes were sad, his mouth curved downwards.

Chaser admitting that he'd made a mistake? He

didn't seem like the kind of guy who owned up to anything unless it was winning.

Leaning closer, I picked up his hand and grabbed the cloth. Wiping at the blood on his forearm, I sighed. What a mess.

"Sloane..."

"Shut up."

"*Sloane.*"

Glancing up, I sucked in a deep breath as I realised how close we'd actually gravitated towards one another.

"There's some things you need to understand," he murmured, pulling my hand away. "But..."

"But what?" I demanded.

"Orders..."

"*Here we go again*," I snorted. "I have no allegiance to Fortitude."

"I do." He stared me down, his eyes burning with anger or desire, I wasn't sure which.

"Is it voluntary?"

He glanced away.

"Chaser..."

"Don't push me, Sloane."

"I see the way you are when you talk about them," I went on. "Your lip curls and your mood goes south... big time. You hate them."

"You don't know anything."

"I know you were shot with wooden bullets and

your arm..." I grabbed his wrist and jerked him towards me. "You—" The words died in my throat as I saw the wound on his arm was gone.

It was gone.

I snatched my hand back, my gaze flying up to meet his.

"Like I said," he muttered, "you don't know anything."

I swallowed hard, all my cocky abrasiveness gone. I was raw and questioning my entire existence, my entire being.

Jerking upright, my knees trembled so bad, I fell against the wall. "It's healed like nothing ever happened," I managed to get out. "*What are you?*"

"It's best you don't know."

"No." I shook my head. "I refuse to believe that. Not after today."

Chaser remained tightlipped and zipped up the first-aid kit.

"Give me something," I pleaded.

"I took a bullet for you." His expression softened. "I took a bullet for *you*, Sloane."

The phantom sound of the bullet ricocheting off the brick wall echoed in my ears, and my resolve cracked. He'd been shot because of me. That bullet was meant for my head. They were hunting me like a feral dog behind a dumpster.

A sob escaped my lips as the gravity of the storm I

was in the middle of hit me. My knees buckled, and I slid down the wall.

I'd almost been killed. I'd almost had my throat slit. They'd tried to get me in my apartment. They'd shot at me. *Who were they?* Faceless monsters that I wasn't sure were *human*. They could be anywhere or anyone.

Chaser sat beside me as tears fell down my cheeks.

"Go away," I said with a sob. "I don't need your crap right now."

He said nothing, nor did he move. He just let me cry. A biker wouldn't sit there and watch a woman bawl her eyes out, attempted murder or not. Chaser wasn't a biker, and he wasn't human, either.

"Sloane?"

"*I'm fine.*"

"Yeah," he whispered. "I'm sure you are."

I didn't know what to do anymore, but the one thing I was certain of was the fact that I couldn't run on my own. Chaser said it himself. He took a bullet for me.

"That bullet wasn't meant for you, Sloane."

My expression faded. "What?"

"Those bullets are meant for someone like me," he said, staring at the floor.

"The blood bag I found in the bin..." I whispered and his gaze flew to mine. "The fast healing. Your cold skin. The way you took down that guy outside the pub. You're strong. *Fast.* You seem to have power over people's minds..." I swallowed hard and wiped my trembling hands over my face. "Please tell me it's not real. Please tell me you're not what I think you are."

"*I can't*," he rasped. His expression twisted as if he were in excruciating pain and was trying to keep in hidden.

"Vampire," I said. "You're a vampire."

CHAPTER 11
CHASER

I felt my humanity begin to creep in as she spoke, telling me all the things she'd noticed about me since we'd met back in Fremantle.

At first, it was a slight tug at the back of my mind, an annoying tick that wouldn't go away. Was it her or me that'd triggered it? I didn't know.

It'd been decades since I'd felt anything other than bloodlust and the thrill of the hunt. Letting it all in was too painful to bear—the longer I left it, the more it would sting—so I tried to clamp down on the returning sensations.

"I'm a vampire, Sloane," I said, confirming her words.

"But... Vampires aren't... You..." She was growing pale, her heartbeat speeding up.

"Aren't real?" I scoffed. "Sometimes I wish it wasn't, but I like being a vampire. I was born for it. My life before..." I trailed off with a scowl and balled my hands into tight fists.

Damn humanity. I wished I could shut it off again, but the floodgates had already burst open, and I had no choice but to ride the tsunami.

"H-how does it work?"

"The things written about vampires are mostly true," I told her. "The fangs, the blood, sunlight, speed and strength, immortality, stakes...but we can also command humans to do things. Some people call it compulsion."

Sloane shuffled away from me an inch. "Like mind control?"

"Yes."

"Have you..." she trailed off, her eyes wide.

"Have I done it to you?" I snorted. "I can't do it to you, so don't get your knickers in a twist." Truthfully, I hadn't tried. Sloane hadn't turned yet, so there was a high chance she had enough humanity that I could if I wanted to.

"Why?"

I ground my teeth for a long moment, fighting the twist of humanity growing inside me. It was about time she knew. I could give her that, at least. "Because you're supernatural, too."

Her whole body tensed. "I'm what?"

Her words came out in a ragged whisper, barely audible except to a vampire. I could hear a pin drop if I listened closely enough.

"There's no easy way to tell you this." I turned to face her. "You're a werewolf, Sloane. Your father is a wolf; the whole Fortitude gang are wolves."

"But— How— Do— *Why?*" Her mouth flapped uselessly. It was the first time she'd been lost for a witty comeback.

"By birth. Maybe people can turn into one, but for you, it's bloodline specific. They go back thousands of years, and there are few who know exactly how far. But I wouldn't know. I'm a vampire."

Sloane let out a strangled moan and began drawing in sharp breaths. "No, I'm not," she said, shaking her head. "There's nothing special about me. I'm a nobody. I don't believe you."

"You're far from a nobody, Sloane."

Her eyes filled with tears. "*I'm a nobody.*"

"Life is easier for nobodies," I drawled. "I don't blame you for wanting to be one."

She ran her hands through her long chestnut locks. "Then why don't I... There's a full moon in a couple of days... I've never..."

"You won't transform," I told her. "You haven't triggered your wolf side yet."

Her eyes widened and I heard the patter of her heartbeat as she began to panic. "Triggered? How... How do I do that?"

"I'm a vampire, Sloane," I said again. "I wouldn't know."

Her breathing quickened. "I'm a werewolf," she

mangled to say. "My father's a werewolf. He sent a vampire to get me. That man... The men at the servo... Who were they?"

I'd given her an inch and she'd taken a mile. How could I be surprised?

"Wolves," I replied. "The two I shot were wolves."

"And the guy at the pub. The ginger..."

"A vampire."

She hugged her arms around her knees. "Were they sent by my father?"

"No." I shook my head. "They were from a rival pack, not from Fortitude."

Her brow creased as her mind ticked over. "They wanted to kill you because you have me?"

I nodded.

"And the vampire wanted to take me." Her gaze met mine. "I'm valuable... Why?"

"I don't ask questions," I lied. It was better she didn't know what fate awaited her outside of Fortitude...maybe inside it, too. If she knew, she'd hurl herself off a cliff.

"You've got to know," she argued.

I did, but I wasn't telling. She took the hint and her expression turned inwards as she thought over everything I'd revealed.

"You're a vampire..." she whispered. "You drink blood."

I rolled my eyes. "Last I checked."

"Do you..." She coughed. "Do you want to drink my blood?"

"Don't tempt me."

Sloane tensed, but she didn't move away. She had some backbone, I'd give her that. Most people would do whatever it took to get away from me.

"Why did you shoot those wolves?" she asked. "If you're strong, why didn't you just use your... uh...your..."

"Fangs?"

She flushed.

"Because I was trying to keep the truth from you," I told her.

"How old are you?"

"You don't want to know."

"How did you become..."

"Never ask a vampire how they turned," I snapped, pushing to my feet. Now that she knew the truth about me, I moved faster than her eyes could follow. It was refreshing, not having to hide.

She gasped, taken aback by my unnatural speed. "Then tell me how you can go out into the sun."

"I had a witch put a spell on me."

"Now you're just taking the piss," she complained.

"It's true."

Her eyes widened. "Bloody hell, there's witches, too? What else is there?"

"Hopefully nothing," I drawled. "The world is

complicated enough." I scooped up the car and room keys from the table.

Sloane tensed. "Where are you going?"

"To get something to eat."

Her heartbeat skipped. "You're going to eat someone?"

"I wouldn't put it like that, but yes." I stalked towards the door. "Don't worry, I'll bring you back something edible."

I returned with a bag of food and my veins full of fresh human blood.

Sloane tore open the bag and began eating the hamburger I'd gotten from the local takeaway like she'd been starving, and for all I knew, she might've been. I'd forgotten humans *and* wolves needed food far more frequently than I did.

I watched her eat with a raised eyebrow. It was messy, just like a wolf. She might not have realised what she was, but her subconscious sure did.

Sloane wanted a way to escape, and so did I. Until now, I thought it wasn't a choice on the table. In a way, it still wasn't. They were still after her, which meant I had to see this through, no matter which way this went.

I was a master at finding people. I knew their tricks. I could find, but I also knew how to hide.

No, I couldn't entertain it. Helping her was bad news. I'd already been shot once.

Sloane sucked tomato sauce off her fingers. "Chaser?"

I grunted. We were already a day behind schedule. Even if we got on the road at first light and made up the distance, we would add another day by tomorrow night. At least we would be going in the right direction. The longer we were out here, the more risk there was.

"I know you weren't supposed to tell me about all this."

I tensed. "Finish your food before you say something you'll regret."

"It's okay," she added. "I won't tell."

Grinding my teeth, my mind rolled over. *I won't tell, I won't tell, I won't tell...* Tell what? That I followed orders down to the letter? Marini hadn't said anything about not telling her about supernaturals.

The moment Sloane was finished eating and had gone to bed, I went outside and changed the license plates on the car. Tomorrow, we were going back on the road to Melbourne.

CHAPTER 12

SLOANE

I didn't want to wake up. Not today.

Still, my eyes opened to a semi-dark room. Either I was done sleeping or something had woken me.

The sound of typing echoed through the motel room, and I rolled over, my mind surfacing into wakefulness.

Chaser was sitting at the table. He was fully clothed, and his hair was damp from a shower. But that wasn't what made me sit up. He had my computer in front of him, the screen glowing as he not so gently smashed on the keyboard.

"What are you doing with my laptop?" I demanded.

"You need to call your blonde friend," he replied, not even bothering to turn around.

"My blonde friend?"

"You need to call her."

"Why?" I groaned and rubbed my eyes. They were full of grit after crying myself to sleep last night.

"She's filed a missing person's report."

"Huh?"

I'd believed Yvette would forget about me quick smart, but here she was going to the cops. Thinking about Mrs. Adelstein and the security footage behind the *Sailor's Arms*, I screwed up my face. Kinda stood to reason someone might report something.

"The sooner, the better, Sloane."

"You smashed my phone," I said. "How am I supposed to call when I've got no phone?"

He tapped the table and kicked the second chair out from underneath it.

Sliding out of bed, I knew I would not like what I saw. He'd had a phone this entire time, along with my money, and it was a glaring indicator to my dependence on him. The illusion I had any say in what was happening was about to shatter, and boy was it going to be spectacular.

A mobile phone was sitting facedown on the table next to my laptop. Looking at the screen, I saw it was plastered with a police report with my face on it. Missing person, indeed.

"You looked through my computer?" I exclaimed.

"Sit down, Sloane."

Sitting, I glanced at him out the corner of my eye. All traces of yesterday's hero were gone. The kind words, the supernatural deep and meaningfuls, the push and pull. He was so closed off, he bore a striking resemblance to a vault in Fort Knox.

Picking up the phone, he turned it on and handed it to me. I stared at the screen, earning myself one of his trademark glares.

"Why didn't you do your mind control thing on her?" I asked.

He didn't bother looking at me. "There wasn't time."

"Well, I don't know her number by heart," I complained. "Nobody knows phone numbers anymore. It's not 1995."

Showing me the laptop screen, my mouth fell open. There was an address book that must've synced from my phone to the computer at some point. There was an entire list of everyone I'd ever called or texted. It felt like he'd glanced up my skirt, the pervert.

"You went through my stuff?"

His eyes narrowed. "Call her, and don't let on about..."

"About what? Because I've got a lot to say about dead bodies, kidnapping—"

"*Sloane.*"

"Fine." Tapping in the number, I pressed the call button and slapped the phone to my ear.

It rang three times before Yvette picked up.

"Hello?"

"Yvette, it's Sloane."

"Sloane! Where are you?"

"I'm around," I replied, glancing at Chaser.

"It's been a week, Slo."

"Sorry. I was busy."

"Busy skipping out on me?"

"It's complicated." Chaser nudged me with his boot.

"I saw the security footage from out back," she began, her speech stilted as if she was reading from a script, and my hackles rose.

"A guy tried to grab me when I went to take the rubbish out," I said, attempting to throw her—and whoever was listening—off the scent. "It was nothing. He was off his face and couldn't even stand up straight. You know what people are like at the *Sailor's Arms*. He ran off, anyway."

"You should've reported it," Yvette complained.

"Maybe, but it was nothing. The cops would've taken a report and never gotten back to me. A never-ending cycle of paperwork with no resolution. Besides, I've had worse. So have you."

"Still..."

I paused, listening to the background noises. There was someone there, heavy breathing and shuffling papers. It wasn't Yvette.

"I'm sorry I worried you," I said after a moment.

"Where are you, Slo? Are you coming back?"

"Nah. I didn't think anyone would miss me." That was partially true. I'd never allowed myself to get too close to anyone considering who my father was. A broken childhood instilled certain fail-safes in my brain.

"I miss you!"

"Well, I'll call you when I get settled. Maybe you can tell me how Brittany's going and all the pub gossip."

"Slo? Where *are* you settling?"

"I don't know yet. I've just gotta find a happy medium, you know? Work, cheap rent, internet access."

"You still studying?"

I glanced at Chaser. "I'm trying to."

"I'm worried about you, Slo."

"You don't have to be. I'm cool. Totally sweet or whatever the kids are saying these days." Chaser made a cutting motion across his neck. "Listen, I've gotta go, but I'll call you when I'm all settled, okay?"

"You better."

"See ya."

Hanging up, Chaser took the cell out of my hands and opened the back. He took out the SIM card and snapped it in half.

"We're in trouble, aren't we?" I asked, watching as he tossed the pieces into the bin.

"What makes you say that?"

"One, you're not making eye contact, and two, that call was totally traced."

Chaser raised his eyebrows and made a point of looking at me.

"There was someone in the background," I replied. "Breathing heavy like a total creep."

"We have to be careful until we get back to Melbourne."

"Do I have to cut my hair?"

He scowled and curled his lip. "What?"

"They do it in the movies. When people are on the run from the cops, they cut and dye their hair. Mainly to avoid security cameras, surveillance, and facial recognition." I flipped my hair over my shoulder and twirled a strand around my finger. "Do you think I'd look good as a blonde?"

"You don't have to change your hair." Chaser stood and crossed the room, gathering our things and shoving them into bags.

I watched him with a blank expression, weighing everything in my mind.

We were in trouble. He knew it and was having a hard time covering it up. Chaser appeared to be torn up about something. *Join the club.*

"We need to go," he barked, throwing my boots at me. "*Now.*"

"Chaser..."

Something in my voice must've slapped him back into reality because he paused, and a little of the guy who'd surfaced the night before shone through.

"Are things going to be better once we get to Fortitude?"

Silence stretched between us. Outside, I could hear

the residents of the motel waking up and moving around. A door slammed, a TV switched on, and something thumped against the wall. Beyond, the sounds of traffic swishing past were muffled by the building at our backs.

Chaser scowled and picked up his bag. "Get in the car, Sloane."

Sighing, I tugged on my boots. Anywhere was better than here, I supposed.

<hr>

Chaser was back behind the wheel, obviously recovered enough to take charge again. Considering he healed so fast, I wondered if he felt pain at all, if the agony was so fleeting that it hardly even registered.

We were headed north again, taking the highway towards the Eyre highway that crossed the Nullarbor Plain and into South Australia.

All I could do was curl into the passenger seat and watch the flat, arid landscape fly by, my mind full to bursting with everything Chaser had told me the night before.

There was nothing I could do about that, either. I knew nothing. I was so far from being in control it wasn't even funny.

"Who are they?" I asked, breaking the three-hour cone of silence.

Chaser glanced at me, then turned back to the road.

"C'mon, what's the harm in telling me?" I complained. "Who are the vampires that after me?"

"Don't worry about who they are," he replied. "Worry about staying alive."

"Someone is trying to kill me, Chaser. So far, there's been two attempts. I can't let it go. Not after everything you told me. I won't go into this blindly."

He remained silent.

"I'm in this up to my eyeballs, and I don't know who you are, let alone what my father wants, because we both know these vampires who are after me are a thinly veiled attempt at sinking his poisonous claws back into me."

"That bullet was the farthest thing from a thinly veiled attempt as you can get," Chaser said.

"Who are they?"

He ground his teeth. It was a wonder he had any pearly whites left in his mouth at this point.

"Who are they, and why can't we disappear someplace together?"

"You need to stop trying to convince me to run away with you."

"I'm not going to stop because I want nothing to do with Fortitude...and neither do you."

"Yet another story you've made up to convince yourself that you have a chance," he replied.

"Pull over," I demanded.

"Not going to happen."

"*Pull over.*"

"Nope."

"Pull over the car before I grab the wheel."

With a growl, he swerved to the side, the wheels flying into the gravel, and slammed his foot on the brake. I was flung forwards, and the seat belt caught and tossed me right back.

"What?" he shouted. "What do you want from me?"

"Do you think you're the only tortured soul in the world?" I asked, seeing red. "Poor Chaser, leading the life of a hired thug. You're powerful *and* immortal, but here you are doing the bidding of a *dog*."

"*Sloane.*"

The warning was clear in his voice, but I wouldn't back down. *I was done.* The back and forth, the false faces, the secrets and lies. It was time to snap him in half and find out what *really* made him tick.

"You hate it," I continued. "You hate working for Fortitude. You're not one of them. You're too good for it."

"It doesn't matter who I am—"

"It matters," I argued. "Either you turn the car around and take me someplace else other than Fortitude, or I walk."

"Sloane, get it through your pretty little head. If you leave and go it on your own, you will be dead before the day is done. You get me?"

"Oh, I get you."

"Then why are you still fighting me?" he exclaimed.

"Because you're taking me to the last place on earth I want to be. Because there's more to you than just a mindless slave carrying out the orders of a werewolf. Because there's something you're holding back."

"You know nothing," he snarled.

Leaning towards him, I stared him straight in the eyes and curled my hands into his T-shirt.

"You think I'm just some dumb girl with an attitude problem," I murmured. "You think I can't handle myself or make rational decisions. You think I need a man to save me. Well, you're dead wrong."

His eyes darkened. "You need to let me go."

"You need to tell me the truth, Chaser. What aren't you telling me?"

"You're walking a dangerous path..."

"*Why?*" I tugged him towards me. "*Tell me.*"

He growled and pulled away, throwing the door open and climbing out of the car. I watched as he paced in front of the bonnet, his fingers pinching the bridge of his nose.

Well, I supposed things were well and truly cracked open now. Might as well go the whole hog and roll around in the ashes.

Getting out of the car, I strode towards him and raised my hand. My palm connected with his cheek and the crack echoed along the empty road. Epic improvisation right there.

Chaser stared at me in shock, rooted to the spot.

The blow hadn't hurt him one bit, but the act had stunned him, nonetheless.

I stared right back, not willing to back down.

I had a feeling things between us would always come to this point. A tense standoff on the side of a road someplace, staring one another down like angry wolves on the border between the absolute truth and mauling each other to death.

Someone was trying to kill me to get to my father? So what?

Chaser practically kidnapped me? So what?

I was a werewolf and didn't know what any of it meant. Someone wanted me for unknown reasons. Other wolves were trying to kill me. The vampires...I wasn't sure if they wanted the same thing, or if they intended to kidnap me, too.

Chaser's eyes began to change, the whites swirling with a blackness that alarmed me. My fight or flight reflex told me to stay still.

Don't move.

Chaser looked at me for a long time before he spoke, but the blackness didn't fade.

"You've fallen headfirst into the snake pit, and you don't even know it," he murmured. "It's better you stay in the dark."

"I passed the point of no return the moment you showed up. Full disclosure, Chaser. That's what I want."

He tensed and the shadows in his eyes began to fade.

"I'm ready," I murmured. "I'll drop the act. I'll stop trying to run away. I'll stop and listen to you. But you have to be honest with me. I want to make my own choices. I want to choose, you hear me?"

"If I go..." He swallowed hard. "If I take you someplace else, it'll never stop. You belong with your own kind."

"I don't care."

"*I do.*"

I tensed, my heart twisting inside my chest. "So the only choice I have is between two evils? You understand you're taking away the one thing I want the most? You get that you're taking away my freedom, right?"

"I'm sorry, Sloane," he murmured. "But if I have to choose between Fortitude or death, I'm choosing Fortitude."

CHAPTER 13

SLOANE

That night, Chaser stopped at a little motel outside some nondescript town on the edge of the Eyre highway. From here, it was an eight-hour drive to the South Australian border.

Since he wouldn't let me drive, we were forced to camp out so he could get a little shuteye. Seemed like vampires needed sleep after all.

Fossicking through my duffel, I took out some clean clothes and set them aside for the morning. Making a pile, I arranged everything else while Chaser banged about the room behind me.

When my hand knocked against the heavy books I'd brought along for the ride, I paused.

I'd already forgotten about my textbooks and the week of lectures I'd missed while we were on our cross-country road trip from hell. Still, I'd carried my work with me on the off-chance I'd be able to catch up at some point. I knew a part of me was still holding onto the life I wanted to have, even though it'd been snatched out of my grasp.

This was one of those crossroad moments, wasn't it? I was perched on a fence that was wobbling underneath my backside, forcing me to choose. If I didn't, it threatened to toss me wherever it pleased.

Glancing at Chaser, I thought about all the things he'd told me. I couldn't quite articulate what it felt like, knowing I was a werewolf but having zero connection to it. It was kind of like a video game where the main character levelled up and was able to face tougher enemies, except I had no idea how to trigger the next level.

Chaser had somehow forced me to see my situation in a different light. He'd given up something when he told me the truth. I wasn't sure what it was yet, but it was something he valued. The way he'd shut down once we'd gotten back into the car was a glaring indicator.

Watching as he unfolded a map and laid it on the table, I raised my eyebrows.

"Wow, I haven't seen a map like that in forever," I said, speaking for the first time since our conversation on the roadside.

Chaser grunted and leaned over the table, studying the lines. There weren't that many of them.

"Is there any good news?" I asked.

"We're stuck," he replied. "There's only one way from here."

"Then we go that way."

"The likelihood of trouble—"

"Is a risk we need to take." I nodded at the map. "Where are we?"

"Here." He jabbed his finger at a point in the middle of nothing. It fit the scene outside, but he could've pointed anywhere, and I would've believed him.

"So, we either go back the way we came or go forwards."

"They'll be expecting it."

"They'll be expecting both courses of action," I shot back. "We just have to deal with it. Be smart. Keep our heads down until we can shake them."

"We go forwards," he said after a moment of deliberation. "Nonstop."

"If that's the way we have to go, then so be it." I sighed. We'd have to at least stop for fuel.

Chaser grunted and sat on the edge of the bed.

Standing over him, I went for the higher ground tactic. I wasn't sure if it would override his vampire aura, but it was worth a shot.

"You know, it would be much easier for me if I knew who we were dealing with," I said.

He stared at me, saying nothing.

"I told you I was ready to drop the 'too stupid to live' act," I said, giving him a pointed look. "But you need to give me something to arm myself with."

"What's the catch?"

"The catch is me having a chance to fight back and not rely on you. If I know who I'm looking for, it might be the difference between living and dying."

Chaser ran his hand over his face and glanced away.

"I can fire a gun."

"I'm sure you can," he said. "Though it won't help much against a vampire."

"But it could if it was a wolf, right?"

He shrugged.

"Chaser, I'm not the kind of woman who just sits back and waits for the cavalry."

He turned his gaze on me, and his eyes burned right through me.

"You know I'm right."

"Fortitude is in something," he said slowly, choosing his words precisely. "Something big. It stretches beyond their normal dealings. This is dangerous stuff, Sloane. Your father saw an opportunity... Now they're coming back twice as hard."

"I knew it," I exclaimed. "Power-hungry son of a b—"

"There's a debt to be paid, Sloane. I'm sorry you had to be dragged into this."

"I'm the payment. Blood for blood," I exclaimed. "After a lifetime of not knowing one another, they think I'm important to him?"

"I'm here," Chaser said, leaning forwards and placing his elbows on his knees. "If he didn't care, I'd be someplace else and you'd be dead already."

"Thanks for the sunshine and rainbows."

"You're welcome."

He spoke plainly for what felt like the first time since we'd met. Like I was an actual person and not a piece of cargo. He was softening towards me, and I wasn't sure how to take it.

"You saved my life twice. It's time to start playing the game." I sat beside him.

"What was your name before?" he asked.

"You're changing the subject. Don't be so blatant."

He raised his eyebrows and waited.

"Didn't my darling daddy tell you?"

He shrugged. "Guess he knew it wasn't important to you anymore."

"Betty," I drawled.

"You're kidding?"

"*Lame.*" I rolled my eyes. "He chose it, not my mum."

"Your mother... You said..."

"I know what I said," I drawled. "He killed her. Not directly, but he may as well have. A little bit of history repeating."

Chaser tensed but didn't ask for an explanation. He was a good soldier. Keeping his mouth shut and his nose out of other people's business were the hallmarks of a career criminal.

"It's just one thing after another," I went on. "This isn't anything new. Not really. Gravitate to my dad, and after a while you'll end up as collateral damage."

"I know."

Maybe it was time to resign myself to the fact I wasn't going to escape all this chaos. Being pulled back into Fortitude business was inevitable now that I knew the truth. If it weren't Chaser and the mystery supernatural hit squad, it would be someone or something else.

"These people..." he began, his tongue loosening. "They could be anyone and anywhere."

"It sounds more sophisticated than just a bunch of vampires and wolves. Those guys at the service station looked like bikers. And that guy who attacked me back at the pub... He was a vampire, wasn't he?"

Chaser nodded. "Appearances can be deceiving. Next time, we won't be so lucky."

I rolled my eyes. Looked like I'd been living in a bubble of false hope if I thought giving him the slip had been a good idea.

I squirmed and leaned back. "They're two separate groups. Why?"

"Vampires and wolves don't mix."

"So, why are *you* working for werewolves?"

"Because I am."

"You're not going to tell me?"

"*No*." He bit back so hard, a little part of me withered and died.

"What now?"

"The safest place for you is with Fortitude. I still stand by what I said to you today."

"The lesser of two evils."

"Yes. It's a matter of survival."

I didn't want to accept it was my only option. What kind of life would I have back in Melbourne, trapped by the whims of my father, the alpha wolf of the Fortitude pack? It still sounded stupid saying it —*wolves and packs*.

"So," I began, my voice thin, "do I just sit around, locked in some room at Fortitude? Do I just go back to the life my mum died to keep me away from?"

"That's up to you and your father."

Great.

Standing, I gave Chaser the dirtiest look I could and rounded the end of the bed. I shucked off my jacket, then kicked off my boots.

"Whatever," I said. "I'm taking a shower."

"*Sloane.*"

"There's something you're not telling me," I said. "About you, your supposed allegiance with Fortitude, and about my werewolf-ness. You've only told me the bare minimum, but why tell me anything at all?"

"I—" He closed his mouth, and his jaw tensed.

"Say it," I murmured. "Just say it, Chaser."

"I care about you, that's why—"

"I don't believe you." I shook my head, shoving down the urge to slam my fist into the wall.

"You're asking me to run away with you," he shot back. "You're asking me to walk away from Fortitude. What you want me to do will put a target on my back. I can't—"

"You're not stuck, Chaser. You can leave, you know. You could choose to take the risk if you wanted it badly enough, but I see you don't. You're too cowardly to walk away from something that's destroying you. *You're a vampire.* You can go anywhere and do anything."

"You don't know *anything* about me," he snarled.

"I know more than you'll ever realise." I backed into the bathroom and slammed the door closed, shutting him out.

Something had happened to Chaser. Something bad, but it didn't make him special. Everyone had their own sad and broken origin story. He could be a thousand years old for all I knew and enslaved by a magic spell. After everything, I wouldn't be surprised.

And to think I'd thought he'd had a secret tumour.

Those rival wolves at the servo wanted me dead. Chaser, too. The vampire at the *Sailor's Arms* wanted me alive. Beaten, but alive. My father wanted me back, not because he cared—I was too smart to think otherwise—but because he needed me for something. I was valuable to the vampires, and the werewolves didn't want them to have me. What Fortitude wanted was still a mystery Chaser wasn't letting me in on.

Was my father going to give me to the vampires? Was I just a commodity to him? *Why?*

For the life of me, I didn't know why I was so special.

CHAPTER 14

SLOANE

The next morning, we were back on the road before the sun had a chance to peek over the horizon.

I leaned against the window, watching the sky lighten and the stars disappear. Red, orange, and gold streaked overhead, though the proximity of danger dulled the beauty.

I didn't like not speaking to Chaser.

Even though he annoyed me more often than not, his silence made me uneasy. The things he'd admitted to last night should've settled some of the gnawing in my chest, but it hadn't. Questions had been answered with words that'd stirred up even more unknowns. About the men who were trying to kill me, about Chaser and his involvement with Fortitude, and about the truth of who I was.

"Have you ever seen the movie *Thelma and Louise*?" I asked sometime between dawn and midday.

"No."

"Because you're Louise, and I'm Thelma." I waited, but he didn't react. "Wanna know why?"

He glanced sidelong at me. "Not really."

"Louise is the levelheaded one," I said, not caring if he wanted to listen or not. I just needed some noise. "She's got the clear-cut plan. Thelma is an abused housewife who goes on a trip with her best friend—that's you—only to become the victim of an attempted assault. Louise saves her by shooting and killing the guy, so they go on this road trip across America to escape the law."

"I can see the parallels, but it's not the same," Chaser drawled.

"Since when do criminals use the word *parallels*." I rolled my eyes. "You're not doing a good job of hiding your educated ex-Special Forces past."

"Who said I was Special Forces?"

"I don't know. Were you?" I gave him a pointed stare, which only earned me another full minute of silence.

Nothing. He didn't even flinch.

"Stop looking at me, Sloane."

I rolled my eyes. "Anyway, as the movie goes along, Thelma awakens as this law-breaking badarse. She robs a gas station, and they blow up a tanker after the driver makes a lewd gesture at them."

He gritted his teeth. "Is there a point to this?"

"I'm not going to peer over my shoulder all day," I said, staring at my reflection in the side mirror. "Or for the rest of this road trip to the seventh layer of Hell. I want a gun, Chaser. Specifically, my gun. I want to be Thelma."

"No."

"Why not?" I was on the verge of pouting and stamping my foot, but I'd already promised to stop the 'too stupid to live through stubbornness' routine. Besides, it wasn't appropriate to give a firearm to a child.

"I don't need to explain myself to you."

"Don't you like me challenging your masculinity?" I asked. "Or is it a vampire thing? Are werewolves the bane of your immortal—"

"*Sloane*." He sighed and tightened his grip on the wheel. "I told you already. I care about you, I do, but it's my job to protect you. Mine alone. You're not making it easy for me."

"Ditto."

I could go on all day and night about how he was wearing a mask. About how he was hiding some big secret about me, Fortitude, and the supernaturals who were hunting us. I could go on about a lot of things, but when it came to me having a gun...? It should be a no-brainer.

"I'm not going to shoot you," I told him.

Chaser cursed and straightened up in his seat.

"What?"

"Fuel light is on."

"We need to stop for petrol?" I glanced out the window, not liking the uneasy feeling the vast nothingness of the Nullarbor gave me. "Out here?"

"I was hoping it would last a little longer," Chaser said. "There's no cover out here."

"Don't you mean, there's zero witnesses?"

He glared at me and continued down the highway. There were roadhouses at regular intervals, so we just had to make it to the next one.

The one we found turned out to be rather modern, and luckily for us, it was mostly empty. Only one other car sat at the bowsers as we stopped, belonging to a woman who was just walking in to pay.

I supposed it boded well for us. Less people meant less chance of being spotted by the elusive enemy. I still had no idea who they were, and the farther we drove, the more it bothered me.

Chaser cut the engine.

"Can I get out?" I asked. "I'm a little hungry, and my backside is numb."

"Stay in the car and get down," Chaser ordered.

Sliding down in the front seat, I grimaced and peered over the top of the dash at the garage beyond. The automatic doors swished open as the woman exited and walked over to her car. A dark-coloured sedan pulled in off the road and turned into a spot by the windows.

Glancing at Chaser, I wondered how he knew what to look for. The notion of detecting a threat through body language was a foreign concept to me, and so was spotting a tail. I'd watched a lot of movies with those kinds of things, but who knew if they were real or not? I always thought a silencer on a gun made the shot go *pew-pew*, thanks to spy shows and James Bond movies. But in reality, it still went *boom* when someone pulled the trigger, silencer or not.

Chaser shoved the nozzle back into the bowser and closed the tank on the side of the car. Tapping the window, he walked across the concrete towards the roadhouse. A moment later, he disappeared through the automatic doors.

Watching the second car, I narrowed my eyes as two men got out. The one nearest was tall and thin with a pointed nose. The other was more robust with a mean look about him.

Both men were wearing tidy jeans and sports jackets with open collar shirts—hardly criminal material. Their car was rather nice, which was why I didn't pay much attention to them at first.

Then, as their gaze turned towards me, I remembered what Chaser had told me the night before. *They could be anyone.*

How did someone tell a werewolf from a vampire? *Was* there a way? They all looked human, until they weren't. I hadn't even seen a set of fangs...yet.

When the men began walking towards the car, I realised I was borderline screwed.

A chill shuddered through my body, and I checked the mirrors. I couldn't be sure they'd seen me, but if I stayed put, they'd find me for sure.

I had to get out of here. *Now*.

I opened the door a crack, just enough for me to slide out, and crouched down on the ground. The sound of approaching footsteps echoed on the concrete, making my stomach roll. I closed the car door softly so the latch caught, then made a break for it.

Crawling across the concrete, I ignored the scraping on my knees and moved between the opposite pair of bowsers. I rose slowly and glanced between the hoses, getting a good look at the men. The taller one cupped his hands against the window and peered inside the car.

"It's empty," he said.

The other guy nodded towards the automatic doors, solidifying my fear.

Chaser.

The men followed him into the roadhouse, and my heart twisted. He was smart, so he'd know something was up, wouldn't he? He had all that vampire super hearing and strength. He'd know they were there with their wooden bullets, right?

Bloody hell, I didn't know. Chaser was an enigma.

Who knew what game he played behind those iridescent eyes?

I cursed under my breath and darted across the concrete and through the doors.

That's right, you idiot, I thought. *Run headfirst into danger, cause that's a smart plan.*

Inside, there were two aisles. One with junk food and magazines, while the other held various bits and pieces of hardware and motor oils. A bank of refrigerators sat along the far wall, full of brightly coloured drinks. The dull sounds of some pop song wailed out of speakers set into the ceiling, but no gunshots or sounds of men fighting greeted me.

At first, I couldn't see anyone else other than an attendant behind the counter.

Sliding down the aisle in front of me, I padded past a row of motor oil, transmission fluid, and other assorted tools and puncture repair kits.

"Where is she?" a man hissed.

Peering around the corner, I stifled a gasp when I saw a knife at Chaser's throat. One of the men had him boxed in, the blade pressed against a very sensitive vein. He was unable to move without causing one hell of a scene with his blood as the main character.

There were two of them... They both came in here together, so where was the other guy?

If Chaser had just given me the gun when I'd asked him...

"There's my girl," a slimy male voice purred behind

me. He'd moved so silently, I hadn't stood a chance. I was a werewolf, *apparently*, but I was still human.

I only had a split-second to react. Grabbing a bottle of transmission fluid off the shelf, I heaved it over my shoulder. The man behind me let out an *oomph* as the heavy container smacked him right in the face. I spun on my heel, grabbed another bottle of something, and swung it with all the strength I could muster.

Five litres of motor oil collided with the man's face, and he stumbled to the side, smashing into the shelving. Bottles flew everywhere as I glanced over my shoulder, checking for Chaser.

The commotion had caused the other man to falter, giving Chaser enough time to disarm him. He twisted and grasped the knife, moving so fast his entire body became a blur, and before I could take a breath, he slammed it home. The blade sank into the man's chest, and he dropped.

Chaser's gaze met mine and he shouted, "*Down!*"

Like we were in some kind of coordinated stunt in an action movie, I ducked as he reached behind his back and pulled out a gun. One shot rang out, echoing loudly in the small space, but one shot was all it took.

Twisting my head, my mouth fell open as I saw the man I'd smashed with the bottle of oil fall onto his back as blood erupted from his chest. Then he began to turn a shade of sickly grey, his veins bulging as his flesh sank inwards.

Gasping, I looked up at Chaser, not quite believing what'd just happened.

He stared back at me for a moment, then his lip curled. Striding across the store, he moved behind the counter and grasped the attendant's shirt. I scrambled after him, wanting to get as far away from the dead bodies as possible.

"Mister," the attendant wailed, holding his hands in the air, "take what you want. Take whatever, just don't hurt me."

"I don't want to hurt you," Chaser said with a snarl. He focused on the man. "You saw nothing. Heard nothing. Some customers came in and paid for fuel and left. The shelf broke and you're going to clean it up. Understand?"

I emerged from behind the shelf, my hair falling into my face. The attendant was staring slack-jawed at Chaser and nodded.

"Where's the security footage?" he asked.

"O-out back."

"Take me." To me, he said, "Stay there."

He dragged the poor attendant from behind the counter, and a moment later, the sound of breaking glass and plastic echoed through the open door. I cringed, my gaze turning to the vampire with the knife in his chest. He was dead, but he hadn't shrivelled up like the other had.

"Sloane." Chaser was beside me, his hand curling around mine.

"Why did he go like that?" I asked, nodding towards the dead vampire.

"That's what happens when a vampire dies. They desiccate."

"Are you going to have to kill the other one?"

He nodded. "He'll heal if I don't."

"But—"

"Sloane," he interrupted, "go wait in the car. I'll handle this."

He didn't have to ask me twice. I glanced at the pooling blood and hightailed it outside and slid into the car.

I could see him moving through the windows as he tidied up the mess, then as he carried out the first body. He held the heavyset vampire like he weighed nothing at all, and that's when I realised just how strong he was.

I was weak. Useless. I'd gotten lucky in there.

The car rocked as he stuffed the body into the boot, and I curled my nose. He retrieved the second and dumped it in as well.

Maybe I could've helped if I were a full werewolf. Maybe that's why he wouldn't give me a gun? I was still human until I turned.

Chaser got into the driver's seat. "That was a really stupid thing to do."

I blinked. "Saving you was stupid?"

"You didn't save me," he replied. "I had it under control."

"No, you didn't," I shot back. "You told me to stay in the car. You know where they checked first?"

He said nothing as he turned over the engine.

"A thank you would be nice," I exclaimed. "Thanks for being smart and getting out of the car, Sloane. Thanks for beating that guy's face in, Sloane. You were a real help, Sloane. Man, you were right when you said you can take care of yourself, Sloane."

"Shut up!" Chaser exclaimed as the car shot out onto the highway. "You're so infuriating."

"I'm infuriating? Look in the mirror!"

"You've got the biggest attitude problem of anyone I've ever met. And I've met some nasty people."

"You bet I've got an attitude. It's a man's world out there, Chaser. You don't know a thing about trying to live in it as a woman, let alone a woman hunted by bloody vampires! Oh, and let's not forget rival werewolf packs!"

"You shouldn't have gone into that roadhouse."

"*Pfft.* Like hell I was going to stay in the car and get kidnapped by another set of vampires. You think you know everything."

"What I know is that we're going to have to stop in the middle of the outback and burn two dead vampires," he raged. "We should already be in Melbourne, but now we have to stop and have a barbecue!"

"Good," I said. "I don't want an audience for my first transformation."

Chaser's entire expression changed. He went from enraged to shocked in under a second.

"Excuse me?" he asked.

"You heard me. I know you've got super hearing, so don't pretend you didn't get that."

He shook his head, his gaze resting on the highway. "I'm not entertaining this."

"You were right. I don't stand a chance...*but I can*."

"You shouldn't have to."

"I want this, Chaser. It's my choice."

His jaw tensed. "You don't understand what you're getting yourself into."

"You've been around werewolves." I twisted in the passenger seat. "*So tell me*."

His face twisted into the painful expression he'd had the other night when he'd told me the truth about him and me. He was wrestling with something unknown, but after a moment, he sighed.

"I'll tell you," he said. "I'll tell you what I know, but after I take care of the bodies."

"Promise?"

Chaser nodded. "I promise."

CHAPTER 15

SLOANE

Chaser turned the car off the highway onto a dirt track that led towards the ocean.

The land dipped a little, but it was mostly flat, the sandy earth covered with low-lying shrubs and trees that'd been battered down by gale force winds.

The coastline along the edge of the Nullarbor was called the Great Australian Bight—it was the bit that looked like someone had taken a bite out of the continent—and the land's edge was kilometres and kilometres of sheer cliffs.

The car wasn't made for off-roading, but Chaser made it work, finding a spot concealed from both track and highway.

I sat in the passenger seat, my bare toes digging into the rough sand while Chaser built a pyre. He flitted around like a hummingbird, moving faster than my eyes could follow.

Then as the sun set, he set it alight, the flames flickering hungrily, sparking with flashes of green and blue from the salt as they caught the dried wood.

The wind tore through my hair, blowing it in all directions and dispersing the smoke. It took the smell with it, and I was thankful. The last thing I wanted was to smell two roasting vampires.

Emerging from the car, I sat on a rock, the stone still warm from the day. To my surprise, Chaser sat beside me, his shoulders hunched.

"You could've gotten yourself killed today," he said.

Images of blood burst through my mind. "But I didn't."

"That's not the point."

"I may not be whatever you are, but I'm capable. I'm not some wallflower who'll wait around for a man to save her. I'm going to turn and be who I'm supposed to be."

"Being in this fight means you will have to kill, Sloane. You won't be able to avoid it. Right now, I'm taking that burden for you."

I glanced at him, but he wasn't looking at me. "So, you do have feelings in there."

"Don't mistake my words for anything other than revealing a harsh reality," he drawled.

A wave of anger pulsed through me, and I scowled. Did vampires have any humanity? Did they remember what it was like to be alive before turning into one of the undead? Did he have a heart? Sometimes I thought he did, even though he was cold and abrasive most of the time.

What a pair we made.

"Liar."

"I have no reason to lie."

"Just admit it," I said, fisting my hands into the front of his T-shirt.

He stared at me and ground his teeth, his body tensing. "*I won't.*"

I knew what he was thinking. If he admitted I was right, it meant he'd dropped the ball. It meant he would've been responsible if I'd wound up dead back at that roadhouse. Chaser was obviously not used to losing.

We stared at each other for a long time, the tension boiling right up to the flood marker of what I could bear.

"The moon is full tonight," I said, breaking free of his gaze. "I want to turn and you're going to tell me how."

The tension bled from his cold body, and he turned back towards the flames. "I don't know how. Wolves first turn during puberty. You're past that."

"Puberty?" I exclaimed. "I'm a grown arse woman!"

As I sat there, stewing in anger, I began to realise what all the fuss was about. My anger faded and the familiar threads of sickly understanding replaced it.

"That's it," I whispered, "isn't it? That's why I'm so special."

Chaser was scowling, resigned that I'd just discovered one of the many truths he'd been trying to keep from me.

"I have a choice."

He swore under his breath. "The moon doesn't control you like the others."

"Why?"

"No one knows," he replied. "They say you can turn at will. Wolves are strongest leading up to the full moon and when they've transformed. They weaken with the waning of the lunar cycle."

"So, if I can change at will, then I'll always be strong?"

"Theoretically."

"Theoretically..." The wind turned, sending the stench of the charred vampires towards us and I pinched my nose.

"Sloane, this is uncharted territory," Chaser went on. "Until you were born, a werewolf like you was a myth. A story passed down through generations so many times, it'd almost become fiction. A werewolf free of the cursed moon. It could be a witch's spell, a curse, nature trying to correct itself... It could be anything. You could be strong always, but you could also be tied to the moon in all but your transformations."

I wouldn't know anything until I triggered my wolf side, and then it was all bets off, but first...

"How does a human turn into a wolf?" I mused. "How…" I trembled as logic set in.

"By breaking every bone in your body," Chaser whispered.

My stomach rolled. I couldn't imagine the pain, let alone being forced to endure it every month for the rest of my life. No wonder it was called a curse.

"The first time will be bad, but it gets better after that, right?" I waited for him to answer, but he was silent. "*Doesn't it?*"

"I don't ask questions."

I didn't doubt him. A vampire in a den of wolves seemed like it'd be an anomaly. "Now I understand why the wolves hate me."

Chaser grunted and I knew there was more to it, but for now, I was tied up in the mechanics of transforming.

"I got you a present." He handed me a bottle of scotch.

I raised my eyebrows and took it off him. "No, you didn't."

He smirked. "Yeah, I lied. It was for me. It helps with the…" he gestured to this throat, "but you're going to need it to take the edge off."

"What do you mean? Alcohol helps you?"

He nodded. "Vampires struggle with hunger. The line between human and monster is thin at best. Alcohol helps with the burn in my throat."

I frowned. "Do I make it harder for you?"

"No, I've had a lot of practice."

His tongue seemed to be loosening, so I decided to take advantage. Learning about vampires was in my best interests…and maybe I'd learn something about Chaser.

"You have to die to become a vampire, right?" When he nodded, I added, "Do you remember your life before?"

He lowered his gaze and took the bottle of scotch from me. I watched him take a long draught and figured his answer was yes.

"We carry memories," he finally said. "Shreds of feeling."

"You don't feel?" That explained a lot.

"We can turn it off." He took another drink. "Everything a vampire feels is amplified. Sometimes it's too much…" He drank again. "Who we were before determines who we are after."

"And who were you before?"

His gaze turned fierce, and I snatched the bottle out of his hand. I'd gone too far, and I could sense him shutting off.

I drank, the scotch burning a trail down into my stomach. "I'm guessing it's different for a werewolf."

"Strength, sight, and smell are the same, though you are bound to a mortal life."

"Emotions?"

"There's a reason why you're quick to anger and a pain in my arse."

Despite our predicament, I laughed. "Bloody hell, how did we get here? Barbecuing vampires and turning into wolves?"

"You don't have to do this, Sloane," Chaser murmured. "You have a choice. There aren't many who can say the same."

Chaser had been turned against his will. I hesitated, then drank some more scotch.

"That's the point," I told him. "Since meeting you, I know this is the only choice I'll get to make."

The only sound that replied to that gem was the wind and the crackle of the fire.

"So how do I do this?" I went on. "How do I get things started?"

"There's no instruction manual," Chaser replied. "The instincts are there...you just have to will it."

"Okay." I didn't understand, but I stood, determined to try. "Don't follow me. I don't want an audience for this."

"I'll wait for you here," he told me. "If you need me, call out and I'll hear you."

I glanced over my shoulder. Chaser was silhouetted by the fire, shoulders hunched with a bottle of scotch in hand.

"You're far more human that you realise," I whispered, knowing he'd hear, then I walked away, fading into the shadow clad Nullarbor Plain.

CHAPTER 16

SLOANE

I walked barefoot away from the fire, the glow behind me.

The moon lit up the rugged landscape, tinting the windswept trees silver, their branches twisted like gnarled bones. It was beautiful, like a magical parallel universe dusted with a canopy of stars.

The wind tore at my hair, blowing strands across my face that caught on my lips. Plucking them free, I took a deep breath. If it wasn't for the roasting vampires, the road trip from hell, and the vampire sitting beside the barbecue somewhere behind me, I would've felt a peace...but my heart beat erratically in my chest at the thought of what I was about to do —*break every bone in my body*.

The moon hung full and bright, a massive orb mottled with shadowy craters.

I thought about the dreams I'd been having about

it since I'd turned thirteen. Werewolves first turned when they hit puberty, but I hadn't. Instead, my teenage years were full of strange dreams and an attitude problem I'd put down to my rough upbringing. Now, I realised it was because I was a werewolf by birth. Cursed by the moon and ruled by the wild instincts of a pack animal.

When I felt like I was far enough away from Chaser, I ducked underneath the skeletal branches of a twisted tree and into a hollow underneath.

I'd thought more about the pain than the mechanics and I decided it might be a good idea to get undressed. Somehow, I didn't think clothing was part of the transformation process.

I folded my clothes into a pile as I stripped, my wind ticking my bare skin, then I sat on a rock, the feeling of the rough stone on my bare arse a little mortifying.

I was sitting in the middle of nowhere, stark naked, trying to turn into a wolf. A week ago, my biggest problem was tending the bar at the *Sailor's Arms* and studying for my exams.

I ran my hands through my hair. *Shit, my exams.*

Looking up at the moon, I said a silent prayer that was full of more swear words than was appropriate.

Will it...

I stared at my hands, imagining what it'd be like to see them sprout fur and morph into paws. What colour would my coat be?

Shaking my head, I snorted. Like it mattered.

Will it...

My wrists cracked, forcing my hands to twist backwards at an awkward angle. Pain stabbed into me like a red-hot poker and I cried out, tears springing to my eyes.

Then my spine curled, snapping and popping like fireworks down each vertebrae. I slid off the rock and fell onto my knees, breathing heavily. I cried out in agony as my arms twisted, then my legs broke, and my knee joints popped out of place.

I collapsed, sobbing and writhing. I had no other thoughts. I'd lost control of my body, the transformation taking over as the wolf within emerged, one agonising bone at a time.

Fur sprouted over my bare arms and legs, covering my face and belly. I twisted, convulsing one last time... then I rose on all fours.

My gaze shifted, the world sharpening as if I were focusing a camera lens. Blurry at first, then it all made sense. The silver landscape I'd seen as a human became more defined—from the rise and fall of the land, the shadows cast by the scrub, the tracks left behind by wildlife, the dusting of stars above, and the glow of the moon.

My paws dug into the gritty earth, and I lowered my snout, sniffing. The aura of salt, dirt, trees, and green things filled my nose...and in the distance, the stench of smoke and charred corpses.

Muscles coiled within me and I ran, leaping and bounding with intoxicating speed. My paws landed sure-footedly, my instincts guiding me across the plain.

I followed the currents, the wind guiding me towards the edge of the world. Ahead, the plain sheered off at a sharp right angle, the cliff falling towards the raging ocean. Skidding to a halt, I gazed over the edge, watching the waves crash against the rocks. They foamed silver and white before fading into the inky blackness beyond.

The wind carried other noises, and between the gusts, I heard footsteps. He was looking for me.

How long had I been running? The freedom was unlike anything I'd known and all I wanted to do was disappear into the wilderness, to never return to Sloane, to be the wolf within...but something tugged at my mind—a warning, a memory—and I turned back.

I wasn't sure what happened next, or how I got from the cliff back to the twisted tree where I'd left my clothes.

I lay flat on my back, my body human, my fur and fangs gone. Above, the moon had lowered almost to the horizon, setting as the night gave way to the rising sun.

I heard my name over the howling wind and sat up. My hair covered my naked breasts and I shivered, my humanity flooding back in a nauseating wave.

"Sloane!"

The wind turned, driving towards me, and I drew

in a deep breath. That's when I smelt it for the first time.

Blood, shadow, death.

Vampire.

When he came out of the shadows, I stared as if I was seeing him for the first time. The man who'd grabbed me at the pub, the man who'd kidnapped me from my ordinary life, and the man who...who was what? As I looked at him, I wasn't quite sure anymore.

Everything was different now.

Chaser stared at me, his gaze dipping slightly before he looked away.

"Are you all right?" he managed to ask.

"I..." I wrapped my arms around myself. My bare skin was pricked with goosebumps, and I was starting to shiver despite the warmth in my skin.

"You were gone all night," he said, picking up my clothes and handing them to me. "I wasn't sure if you were coming back."

I clutched my T-shirt against my chest, my entire body tingling with heightened sensations.

"Neither did I," I whispered.

Chaser knelt beside me, his eyes glowing mysteriously as the first sliver of dawn touched the horizon. "How do you feel?"

"Alive," I managed to say. "I feel *alive.*"

CHAPTER 17

SLOANE

I sat sideways in the passenger seat of the car, my arms wrapped around my middle, watching Chaser scatter the ashes of the pyre.

Every nerve ending in my body screamed at me, both from the aftermath of my first transformation and from the new sensations I was experiencing.

My vision was sharper, scents were more defined, and my emotions were more stable than they'd ever been. It was like a piece of my brain that I hadn't known I was missing had clicked into place, and I was complete. All the pathways in my head ran smoothly, the temper that usually rose when I was exhausted had mellowed all the way to zero, and I was left with a calm sense of acceptance.

Overhead, the sky was turning. Another day was here, and we were still in the middle of nothing and nowhere. I'd lost count of how many days Chaser and I had been on the run, tied together by some unknown conspiracy.

"Sloane?"

I blinked, raising my head. Chaser stood before me, and my nose filled with the odd scent that seemed to follow vampires around. I couldn't quite place what it reminded me of, but the image it conjured in my head was one of the shadow and death that went with being a supernatural predator of the night.

"You smell strange," I told him.

His lips quirked. "So I've been told."

I rubbed my jaw. "I feel like I've been shoved through a meat grinder."

"Take it easy for now," he told me. "I'm not sure how long your strength will be around for. If it's tied to the moon, then it'll only be for today."

Looking up at him, I squinted as the first rays of the sun shone over the horizon. "Are we leaving?"

"We need to get back on the road. Cross the border."

I nodded and turned in the seat, kicking my feet into the footwell. He closed the door, the sound ringing in my ears, and he got in the driver's seat.

Leaving another two bodies behind hadn't helped our chances of reaching Melbourne without being pulled over by the cops or being tracked but getting out of Western Australia was the first step at wiping the slate clean.

Honestly, I didn't even know where we were

anymore. This stretch of the Eyre highway, every motel room, and every sunrise was the same as the last. At this rate, I was sure our road trip would never end.

The murky dawn morphed into daylight, and we didn't speak. The car seemed to be a dead zone for feelings, and after last night, neither of us made an effort to define what'd happened.

Leaning my head against the window, I stared into the side mirror, half looking at myself with my blue aviator sunglasses and half looking at the road in our wake. A truck sat a few car lengths behind us, but I couldn't make out anything else. The mirror was too small.

Several dead bodies had been left in our wake, I'd been attacked, shot at, threatened, I'd turned into a wolf, and I was surprisingly mellow about the whole thing. Desensitised, like I knew it was going to happen. Like it was supposed to be *normal*.

I was ten when the first dead body dropped into my life. Sometimes, you've just gotta turn off all the bits inside you that care to get through the storm called life. I didn't know if it made me a survivor or a fruitcake, but it was what I'd always done.

We went over a bump and my head cracked against the window. I winced as the blow vibrated through my entire body.

Chaser glanced at me. "You okay?"

I looked at him, hyperaware of the fact that I ached

everywhere. My transformation hadn't been as smooth as I'd imagined, and I wondered if it'd get any easier. If I didn't have to change, then maybe I'd just stay human... but I'd miss out on the exhilarating freedom of running as a wolf. It was a trade-off of epic proportions.

"I'll survive," I replied, my voice hoarse. "At least until we get to Melbourne."

His jaw tightened, but he didn't glance away from the road.

"You let me turn, which will give me a chance..."

"But it's not enough."

"No," I muttered, looking out the window.

The road noise was the only sound between us. By the looks of it, Chaser wasn't used to whispering sweet nothings or apologising.

"You're handling this incredibly well," he managed to say.

"Keep going on like that, and I'll start to believe you actually care about me."

"I already said I did."

"Yeah, but I didn't believe you."

"What about now?"

I laughed and shook my head. "You sound like a clingy boyfriend."

He grunted. "What was it like growing up? Now you know what you are, does it make sense?"

"You really want to know about my messed-up childhood?" I asked, raising my eyebrows.

"You wanted me to give up everything for you a couple of days ago. Maybe I need a reason."

I froze. What in the world was going on here? I studied Chaser's profile and worried my bottom lip with my teeth. So all that hostility was his shield, not his identity. *Interesting.*

"Was our D&M by the bonfire that good?" I asked.

"Huh?" He glanced at me before turning back to the road.

I shook my head and played with my hair. He knew exactly what I was talking about, the crafty bastard.

"I didn't know any different," I said, deciding to answer his question differently. He was fishing, so I was going to tear the entire rod out of his hands and pull him into the water. "I thought I was like every other little girl I went to school with. I didn't know I was a wolf, but I knew something was up with my father. Mum was great about keeping me away from the truth—a real master at hiding the crime and violence he was into." I snorted and picked at the hem of my T-shirt. "Dad was hardly around. I got the odd birthday present, but it was never consistent. It wasn't until I was older that I realised who he was and what my mother had done for me."

Looking back, I knew I was too young to understand all the signs—Dad's absence, Mum's broken arm, her cuts, and bruises. The comings and goings at all hours of the night, the hushed whispers.

"She put on a brave face," I murmured. "And it was all for me. I was half him, but I was half her, too."

"She protected you," Chaser said.

"From everything. After she was gone, I came to realise just how much pain she shielded me from. It was all my fault. Now I understand she knew I was a werewolf and kept me close to the pack so I'd have that support when the time came. If I wasn't born, then she would've been long gone."

"You can't blame yourself for her decisions...or your father's."

"We all make our choices, Chaser. Mum made hers, and so did my father. He knows how I feel about him, right down to the last wart. My opinion will never change. I don't want to see him, even though he has all the answers about what I am."

"He wants to save your life now—"

"Don't you dare defend that man," I snapped. I sat back in the passenger seat and kicked my feet up onto the dash. "He wants to save my life to save his pride and line his bank account. I'm not his daughter, I'm a commodity. *The werewolf who can change at will.*"

Chaser fell silent, and I didn't have the heart to look at him. I was stuck between my desire to escape a terrible fate and the truth about who I was. I knew what I was asking him to do was just as bad. For him, it was a choice between repaying his mysterious debt to Fortitude or betraying my father for me...a stranger.

We'd had one night of him softening towards me, but ultimately, nothing had changed. Nothing at all.

Knowing it tore my heart in two.

"Did you know her?" I asked. "Did you know me?"

"No," he whispered. "I didn't."

I wasn't sure if that was the truth, but did it matter? The past was long buried.

"They slit her throat, you know," I murmured, watching the blur of scrub streak past outside.

The creak of leather signalled Chaser had tightened his grip on the wheel. The sound was louder than normal, my wolf ears zeroing in on the minutest of details. "She was lying on the kitchen floor in a pool of blood."

"Sloane, you don't have to—"

"Did he tell you how she died?" I asked.

"It's not my business."

"I was told it was a home invasion, that some bad guys had broken into our house while I was at school and attacked her. I sat at the police station, a ten-year-old girl, and waited for my dad to come get me. The dad who was never there, but who was all I had left... and he never did. I never heard from him again." Until Chaser had sauntered into my life, but there was no point in saying it. "At least I was spared from finding her, but I knew it wasn't a random attack. Even at ten, I understood...and now? Who really killed her, Chaser?"

His jaw tensed. "I don't know."

"Was it vampires? Werewolves? Were they looking for me?"

"*I don't know.*"

I glared at him but he never took his eyes off the highway. Maybe he didn't know...or maybe he was good at lying.

I snorted and sat back in the passenger seat. "She sacrificed everything for me, and they killed her before I was old enough to transform...though she never knew I wouldn't. It was all for nothing. We could have disappeared. She could be alive right now."

The silence was painful this time. Restlessness threatened to overwhelm me, and I tensed in an attempt to stay still.

Finally, I felt Chaser's hand on my thigh, his touch icy cold. "I won't let anything happen to you."

"Yeah, right."

My head fell against the window, the fire in my soul dampening. Which way was up? Should I listen to my heart or my head? *Besieged on all sides.*

We crossed the border without issue. The only thing that was in our way was a biosecurity check. Any fruits, vegetables, and honey had to be tossed, but since we had none, we were waved through with barely a cursory glance.

We stopped at yet another roadside motel that night, this time firmly in South Australia.

I watched Chaser as he roamed around the room, checking the locks on the windows and looking in all the cupboards. He opened the bathroom door, turned on the light, and scanned that, too.

"Are you hungry?" he asked.

"Are you?" I made a face. "I've noticed you get *hangry* when you're running low on blood."

"*Sloane.*"

"Why don't we keep driving?" I asked, sitting on the end of the bed. "If we're in that much trouble, wouldn't it be easier to, *you know*...go all the way?"

Chaser grunted, doing his best tall, dark, and silent treatment impersonation. It seemed the warm and caring vampire I'd met out on the Nullarbor Plain had disappeared again, and the cold, calculating predator was back.

"Tell me the truth, Chaser," I demanded, my heart still raw from our deep and un-meaningful conversation in the car.

"We've had enough truth talking already."

I scowled, watching as he stood before me and glared back just as hard. Talking to this man was like flicking a light switch on and off. One second, he was calm and caring, and he was a ball of rage the next. *What war was he fighting inside?*

Then I remembered what he told me about vampires and their humanity. They could turn it off so they didn't have to deal with the pain of what they'd become. Chaser had turned off his humanity...but it was coming back. That was it, wasn't it?

If I got him to feel again, maybe he'd see that taking me to Fortitude was a bad idea...for the both of us.

"For once in your miserable life, *say what you feel*," I declared.

Chaser snarled, and his hand shot out so fast I wasn't able to dodge him. His fingers dug into my skin as he yanked me up off the bed.

"You want to know what I feel?" he asked as I trembled. "I feel this uncontrollable rage when I look at you, Sloane. You drive me *insane*."

My heart pounded in my chest as his words washed over me. I should be afraid of him; I knew it was logical to want to run right now, but I couldn't.

"You won't hurt me," I told him.

"*Stop lying to yourself.*"

"I don't need to lie, Chaser. I know what I am now. I know who I want to be...but can you say the same for yourself?"

His grip loosened. "I've started something..." he murmured, "something I don't think I can stop."

"Your humanity."

He stared at me, his iridescent eyes sparkling.

I doubted everything about him. I was looking for flaws in his perfect exterior that would come out and break my heart when I wasn't looking. I wanted to believe this was going to end well, but it wasn't. That was the problem.

At the end of this road was nothing. Nothing at all. Unless... No, there was no unless. There *was* nothing.

Call it stubborn pride, call it a death wish, call it whatever you want, but I wanted to win.

"You want to know what I feel when I look at you?" I asked.

"I don't need to know."

"I see a troubled man who's trapped in a web of violence and lies. A man who believes he can't escape."

His eyes turned dark, the whites fading as his vampire side rose. "*Shut the hell up.*"

"What does my father have on you, Chaser?"

"I'm warning you, Sloane," he rasped. "Just because I allowed you to transform out there, doesn't mean you're entitled to know things about me. I never asked you to share your sob story."

"My sob story?" I scoffed. "I never once asked for sympathy, Chaser. A little understanding, yeah, but *never* sympathy."

"I know what you're trying to do."

"*Good.*"

"It won't work. *I don't want it.*"

We didn't touch. We didn't speak. He was an inch away from bearing his fangs, and I was on the breaking point of testing out my newfound strength.

It was clear I'd lost the battle, but at least I'd gotten a glimpse of the man Chaser used to be before he lost his humanity. It was a stark reminder of all the things that would be taken away from me once I was shoved over the threshold of the Fortitude compound.

I lay on the bed, the events of the last few days finally catching up with me.

Staring up at the popcorn ceiling, I studied the shadows with a sense of exhausted melancholy. "I really think this is Stockholm syndrome."

Chaser grunted, though I wasn't expecting an answer at all.

I rolled away from him, curling up on my side. He wanted to control me, but I was uncontrollable. I was a whirlwind of fury. *I'd show them all.*

Who was Chaser? I didn't really know anything about him, especially when he said things like that. How could I feel anything for a shadow?

Definitely Stockholm syndrome, I thought. *For sure.*

CHAPTER 18
CHASER

I sat on the edge of the bath, scowling at my reflection in the mirror above the basin.

Running my finger over the scar on my jaw, I shoved away the memory it conjured. I had my fair share of scars from before, though the ones I'd gotten after I'd turned had healed before they left a permanent mark. Those I could forget.

Pain wasn't something that usually bothered me. I'd learned how to manage it a long time ago while out on a job. I'd been shot, knifed, concussed, bruised, and beaten. People did stupid things when they were desperate and on the edge of losing everything. They attacked, sometimes in the worst possible way.

It wasn't only supernaturals I hunted. Humans had their fair share of run-ins with Fortitude, but it didn't mean their bite stung any less. I couldn't go inside their homes for one—I had to be invited in.

Rubbing my jaw, I glanced through the crack in the bathroom door.

Sloane was moving around in the other room, fussing with the doona on the creaky bed. It was hot outside and the room had little ventilation, but she was a full werewolf now—and her senses needed time to adjust.

When she sensed me staring, she turned and padded the three steps from the bed and nudged the bathroom door open.

She was mad at me, but it was nothing new. She was always enraged about something, though her transformation had mellowed her out some.

"Are you okay?"

I nodded.

"Do you need something to eat?"

"Not yet."

She looked me over and pursed her lips like she was desperate to ask me something.

"Out with it," I told her, narrowing my eyes.

"Were you shot before?" she asked. "I noticed a scar on your side...and another one under your jaw. Was that a knife?"

"Something like that."

She scowled when I offered no more commentary.

"I'm not like them," I said, tensing as she moved to leave.

"I'm not so sure about that."

I glanced at her, but her eyes were downcast, her

hair shielding most of her expression from me. She'd let out a lot of heavy emotional baggage so I couldn't blame her. Still, some long-dead part of me was beginning to wake up and give a damn.

"Sloane—"

"There," she said, forcing a smile as she wrenched the doona off the bed. "All better. That thing was scratchy as hell."

I didn't know what I was going to say. Was I going to comfort her? Tell her everything was going to be fine? I couldn't do that. Even if I said it aloud, she would see right through me. Sloane was more switched on than she realised. She was cool, calculating, stubborn, intelligent... Hated to say it, but she reminded me of her father.

"You should try to get some sleep," I told her. "You went through a lot last night."

I couldn't promise her a happy ending. I couldn't promise her anything at all.

She sighed and climbed into the bed, flicking the bedside lamp off as she went. Pulling the sheet over herself, she turned and buried into the pillow.

I glanced at my reflection once more before turning off the bathroom light.

Sleep was the furthest thing from my mind, so I moved like a shadow to the window and peered through the gap in the disgusting mustard-coloured curtains.

The motel parking lot was quiet.

A few cars were parked outside their respective rooms, all of them towards the front of the complex. We were the only occupants at the rear, but I still heard the muffled sounds of people moving around inside, the odd conversation, and the mumbling of a television or two. A semi-trailer roared past on the highway, rumbling off into the distance, followed by a car.

Sensing no danger, the tension in my shoulders relaxed a little.

We had a choice of which way to go now. There was more than one road through to Victoria, and multiple forms of transportation—bus, train, rental cars... Maybe we could get a train in Adelaide. It would be the last thing they'd expect.

It would add another day to an already overdue job, but it was for Sloane's safety. I didn't know how close they were, and I couldn't risk losing her before getting her back to Marini.

That was all it was, wasn't it?

"Chaser?"

Sloane's sleepy voice echoed behind me, and I leaned my head against the window.

The sound of rustling blankets signalled she'd climbed out of bed, and then she was behind me, moving as silently as a panther in the darkness. Her hands were warm to the touch as she rubbed her palm over my arm.

I didn't have the heart to push her away.

"I can't sleep," she said. "I'm too wound up."

I grunted.

"Is it a wolf thing?"

"Probably."

She let her hand slip away. "Can I ask you something?"

"Depends on the question."

She opened her mouth to speak, but closed it, her brow creasing. Sitting on the edge of the bed, her fingers worried the threadbare sheet.

I waited, hoping she'd give up, even though I knew I wouldn't be that lucky.

"I'm trying to understand," she managed to get out, "how things work. How I'm supposed to feel, what I'm supposed to be able to do. I'm trying to understand the vampires that're after us... Know thy enemy, right?"

She was hedging around what she really wanted to ask, and I sighed. "What do you really want to ask me, Sloane?"

She worried her bottom lip, then asked, "How long have you been a vampire?"

There was no harm in telling her. "Since 1891."

"One hundred and thirty years?" The shock was clear on her face, even though she tried to hide it.

"It all starts to feel the same after a while," I told her. "Don't get hung up on it."

"How long have you been working for Fortitude?"

"Almost as long as I've been a vampire." After a century, it was the only life I remembered. The shreds of what I left behind were just that, broken pieces that didn't fit together.

"They've been around that long?"

"There's a reason they're the most powerful pack on the East Coast."

"Is that why can't you leave?"

Of all the questions she could've asked at that moment, it was the last I wanted to hear.

"I just can't," I replied, looking back out the window. The stars were disappearing.

"Explain it to me."

"I'm indebted to them," I said, my jaw tensing.

"Why?"

I felt her hand wrap around mine and I hated her for it. It was as if she knew how to get to my humanity and was doing everything in her power to manipulate it out of me.

"They did something for me that I couldn't do myself." My voice was strained. *Thin*.

"And in return, they branded you into slavery," she whispered, caressing the tattoo on my thumb.

I wrenched my hand away. She didn't understand how true her statement was.

Sloane turned her head and glanced up at me, her big eyes glittering in the silver light of dawn.

"What are we going to do?" she asked.

It was a loaded question, and I knew her mind hadn't changed about our destination. She was still trying to convince me, hoping our changed dynamic had swayed me.

"For now, we head towards Adelaide," I replied.

"For now? After everything you've told me?"

"Sloane, *please*." I clenched my fists, my conviction wavering. "If you keep trying to manipulate me, you'll regret it."

"*Fine*, we'll got to Adelaide." She jerked backwards and crawled into the bed. "*For now*."

CHAPTER 19
SLOANE

I t was the second day after I'd turned.

We were on a highway to hell, *literally*, and it wasn't at all like the song.

I hadn't spoken to Chaser since we left the motel. There was nothing to say that had any hope attached to it, so why bother? My spirit was shrivelling up and dying the closer we got to Melbourne...and so were my hopes that he'd change his mind and help me escape.

I dozed, the heat inside the car sending me into a restless sleep.

It was midmorning when I realised we'd left the main road and were speeding down a dirt track. We went over a bump, and I knocked my head against the window. I scowled as I rubbed my temple.

Chaser turned off the engine.

"What are you doing?" I asked, images of being

murdered and thrown into the water flashing through my mind.

"Get out of the car, Sloane."

"Why?"

"You've been sulking all morning."

"Have not." I totally had, but I wasn't going to admit it to him.

"Get out of the car."

I rolled my eyes and unclipped my seat belt. *Always with the biting commands.*

Opening the door, I was slapped in the face with a wall of heat, and I felt sweat pool in my pores, ready to erupt and soak me through.

Standing, I slammed the car door closed behind me and walked over to the side of the dirt road. The sky stretched on and on, blue like the colour of my mood. Stepping up onto a boulder, I looked down at what I'd thought was a valley and sighed.

A lake stretched out before me, bordered by rocks, orange-tinged dirt, and scrappy bushes that looked half-dead. The water was pretty enough with its turquoise hue and promise of washing off the sweat that was already running down my spine.

"It's not very appealing," I said, shielding my eyes from the sun. "What are we doing here?"

"We need a break."

I raised my eyebrows and snorted. "Aren't you afraid of our murderous friends catching us out in the open?"

"I'm not afraid," he said, not even twitching. "They'll anticipate our route, but they won't know we've stopped here."

"Not unless they stuck a GPS tracker on the car," I drawled. "Or a witchy thingamabob."

Chaser gave me a look, and my mouth fell open.

"There's no such thing!" I hesitated and my eyes widened. "*Isn't there?*"

"We'll know soon enough," he replied with a smirk.

Turning my gaze back onto the water, I wiped my forearm across my brow.

"C'mon," Chaser said before climbing over the rocks.

Following him, we made our way down to the lake, clambering over the scrappy shoreline until our boots hit the sandy bank. I perched on a rock and listened to the water lapping on the shore, allowing my mind to wander in the calmness. Nothing stirred apart from us and the current coursing through the lake.

"Do you think there's fish in there?" I asked, my voice sounding loud in the silence.

"I think the sun is getting to you." Chaser glanced at me, perplexed at where my thoughts had taken me.

"There are lots of things getting to me..." I mused. "I need to write a list to remember them all."

Staring into the lake was like staring into a void, and I felt a surge of adrenaline hit me square in the chest.

"Give me the car keys," I demanded, holding out my hand.

Chaser narrowed his eyes and didn't move.

"I'm not going to drive away or anything. I just want something out of my bag." I wiggled my fingers.

He sighed and leaned forwards so he could take the keys from his pocket. Handing them to me, he gave me a pointed look. "If you try anything, just remember that I can move faster than you can blink."

"*Whatever.*" I snatched them from him and sauntered back up the rocks.

Something had definitely changed between us if he was giving me access to a bonafide escape route and trusting I would come back. I didn't believe him when he said he cared—I just thought he was telling me what I wanted to hear to get me to shut up—but what if he was telling the truth? What if Chaser actually cared? As in, *feelings* kind of cared.

Shivering as I opened the boot, I kept a tight grip on my heart.

In a perfect world, we would run away together.

In a perfect world, I would be able to finish my degree.

Taking out my political science textbook, I stared at the cover, running my finger over the coloured Post-It notes I'd stuck in the pages. They marked important things I was supposed to remember—quotes, facts, ideologies. The scientific study of governments and their politics and policies; otherwise known as the subtle art of bullshitting your way into a position of power.

Why was I still carrying my books around? The moment Chaser turned up at the *Sailor's Arms* was the moment the life I was trying to make for myself dissolved into a dumpster fire. Then the part where I turned into a wolf cemented it. How could I go back knowing what I knew about the world? Vampires, werewolves, *witches*. I couldn't.

Slamming the boot closed, I locked the car and clambered down the rocks, my boots scraping all the way to the water's edge.

When I came back into view, Chaser straightened and watched me with interest.

Staring out across the lake, I clutched the textbook against my chest. This felt like one of those pivotal moments in a *Choose Your Own Adventure* story. One path would lead me to certain death, one would be fraught with danger, and another would transport me right to the happy ending. I didn't know which fork I was about to take, but I knew I couldn't go back.

Twisting to the side, I swung with all the strength I could muster and hurled the book into the air. It flew with surprising height and speed, then cannonballed into the lake, hitting the surface with a slap. The impact sent water everywhere, giving away that my werewolf strength had stuck around after the full moon had subsided...at least a little.

"What did you do that for?" Chaser asked, raising

an eyebrow. "I thought that book was important to you?"

"I've been fooling myself," I said, watching the water rise and fall in miniature tsunamis around the impact zone. "Thinking I could have this amazing life if only I believed... It's a lie. No one's going to give me a medal for participation in the human race." I threw my hands into the air. "*I don't even belong to the human race anymore.*"

Sitting beside him, I sighed, not in the least surprised when he had nothing to add to my heartfelt declaration of despair.

"Can we pretend?" I asked, my cheeks heating with embarrassment. "Just for today?"

Chaser frowned, his brow creasing. I caressed his stubbled jaw, my heart aching. In a way, it felt like goodbye. I was giving up my dreams and resigning to a fate I couldn't escape. Betty was making a comeback, and Sloane was crawling into her coffin.

He didn't move away at my touch. He stayed frozen in place like an elegant marble statue with glowing hazel eyes.

"Just for a few hours..." I whispered.

"Just for a few hours..." Chaser echoed.

"I don't get you sometimes."

"I thought we were pretending?"

"The only thing we're pretending is the nature of our road trip," I retorted. "This... The way I feel when we're together... I'm not pretending."

He said nothing, which didn't surprise me.

"I have no idea where we are anymore," I said, staring up at the clouds. "I lost track somewhere around the border, but that already feels like it happened a week ago."

"That was yesterday," he drawled.

"You're taking the long way on purpose."

"Yes...and no."

"You're just trying to shake the tail of our mysterious pursuers," I muttered, my heart cracking directly down the middle.

Chaser tensed but didn't offer any more of his mysterious thoughts. He really was pretending then.

The lake had swallowed my future but hadn't saved me from my fate. A werewolf who could turn at will, hunted by vampires and wolves alike. Why? *What was the point?*

"All glory is fleeting," Chaser whispered like some kind of mantra.

So was love, by the looks of it. Flirtation, companionship, trust... It was all as fleeting as a fart in the wind. One pungent whiff and it was torn away in a stiff breeze so abruptly, you were never quite sure if you'd truly smelt it at all.

"Is this unrequited?" I asked, knowing I was giving him an ultimatum. "Am I wasting my time?"

"Are we still pretending?"

I tensed. God, I was such a moron.

I'd gone and gotten feelings for a vampire with over

a century of emotional baggage—baggage that he'd avoided by turning off his humanity. I was a lost cause.

"Forget about it," I murmured, looked out across the water. "Forget about everything."

CHAPTER 20
CHASER

I stared at the lake and the gentle ripples on the surface, but I didn't see it. Not really.

Everything Sloane and I were doing was borderline suicidal, and it had nothing to do with the vampires on our tail.

I glanced at her, fighting between telling her everything and saving her from a lifetime of punishment.

I hadn't expected her when I'd walked into that seedy pub or the feelings she'd stirred up since, and it felt like a betrayal to those who came before.

Don't disappoint me, Chaser. You know what happens when you do. Marini's words came back to me with startling clarity. I was so screwed.

"Sloane."

Her chin tilted up, and when her gaze met mine, I could see all the things she was trying to hide.

She didn't want to be like her mother—ending up tied to a man just as bad as her father had been. I rolled with Fortitude, and no matter my reasons, it was all the same to her. She'd done everything in her power to escape that life, and here I was, delivering her back to it.

She was pushing me away without knowing the truth. I didn't have it in me to explain, either. I wasn't even sure she'd understand.

Once our road trip was over, the fantasy would dissolve and be nothing but a memory. I would never see her again, she would never forgive me, and I would go back to the same mindless slavery I'd been living for the last century.

"What?" she asked, glaring when I didn't answer right away.

"You can't tell your father about us."

Her eyebrows rose.

"He'll kill me on the spot, and I'm not ready to die just yet."

"You said that without even twitching," she drawled. "Just when I think I've got you pegged, you ruin everything."

"So?"

"So, you just keep breaking my heart."

I frowned and turned my attention back to the lake.

"You're doing it again."

Pushing to my feet, I tossed her boots in her general direction.

"Put your boots on," I commanded, my mood souring. "We're going."

She opened her mouth, and I turned before she could speak. I didn't want to hear it.

I didn't want to hear anything.

CHAPTER 21

SLOANE

I spent the rest of the afternoon sulking—for lack of a better word.

We were back in the car, my Poli Sci textbook floating somewhere in a lake behind us, and I was still drowning in an emotional limbo the size of the outback.

We were driving through a long, flat expanse of nothingness. We were alone. No other cars or trucks had passed us for some time, and if I had it in me to pretend, then maybe Chaser and I would be the only two people left on the planet. I wished the world had ended and everyone else was gone.

I could do it. I could survive in a world like that. The brutality of it was more romantic than the life waiting for me back at Fortitude.

Alone in a long, flat expanse of nothingness. It was an epic metaphor for my current state of mind. Our pitstop back at the lake had been magical...until Chaser had switched off again.

Push too hard and you could lose everything. Those were some words of wisdom right there.

"I wish you'd tell me what is going on," I said, studying the horizon. "It would make me feel a lot better."

"You keep asking, and I keep saying nothing," Chaser drawled.

"Don't remind me. I feel like I'm on a merry-go-round I'm not allowed to get off."

"Full disclosure?" he asked, raising an eyebrow.

My hopes raised. "*Full disclosure.*"

"We're being followed."

"Huh?" I twisted in the seat and looked out the back window. Sure enough, a black car was trailing us. It was a fair way behind, so I couldn't see who was driving or how many people were inside, but it was there. "How do you know?"

"I've been watching them for the past hour."

"An hour? Why didn't you say anything earlier?"

Chaser grunted. "Because you don't need to know the details. You just need to sit there."

"If that's what you think I'm going to do, you haven't learned a single thing about me," I muttered. "I didn't turn into a wolf to sit on my arse."

They were here for me. It didn't make me feel any better that Chaser was here with his macho alpha bravado. He'd already killed four supernaturals to save my life, but this time was different. We were on an open road in the middle of a dust bowl.

So much for taking the back roads to shake them off our tail. *What a place to die.*

"So what do we do?" I asked, scowling. "Outrun them? Turn and fight?"

"We're on a secluded highway, and the closest town is kilometres away. We can't outrun them in this car," he replied. "And this isn't the Wild West."

"So we're screwed?" I turned, watching the dark-coloured car loom behind us.

"That's a matter of opinion."

"That's just *great*. Who are these guys? Vampires or wolves?"

He sighed. "I'm a vampire, not Superman."

I felt the car slow and my heart jackhammered in my chest. "What are you doing?"

"They're gaining on us," he replied. "They're making their move."

"*Shit*." I turned and recoiled when I saw the black car quickly close the gap. "Chaser, I don't like this..."

"Stay calm, and do what I say," he commanded.

I didn't mind his alpha mode right now. If it got us out of this alive, then he could turn the dial right up to a million if he wanted.

"Sloane?" He glanced at me, then at the rearview mirror.

"Yeah?"

"Hold on."

The car lurched as we were rammed from behind. My head snapped forwards, and I jammed my palms on the dash to steady myself.

"Tighten your seat belt, and cross your arms over your chest," Chaser commanded. "If we roll, it'll protect you."

I swallowed hard and did as he said, my hands shaking. "*Chaser*..."

"It'll be okay," he murmured, glancing in the mirror. "It'll be okay."

I sucked in a sharp breath and held on for dear life, putting all my trust in him, the man I wanted. I'd used the word love a few times in the confines of my own thoughts but never out loud. Did I want to say it? Did I want him to know? Was love what I really felt for him or was it just *Stockholm syndrome*?

It was so not the time for an existential crisis.

Movement caught my gaze, and I looked past Chaser, right into the eyes of a man in the other car. They'd flanked us, and now they were right there, and the man in the passenger seat was aiming a gun out the open window at us.

"*Get down!*" Chaser roared.

I slid down in the seat, screaming as the driver's side window shattered. We swerved to the side as the black car sideswiped us, scraping metal jarring my ears. Chaser wrenched the wheel, trying to break away, then he jammed his foot on the brake before accelerating hard.

I flew forwards, the glowing red taillights of the black car filling my vision as I was flung backwards. Tyres squealed as the other car braked, and before Chaser could correct our forward motion, they clipped us.

The nose of the car went up in the air, and we spun. I screamed, unable to hold on to my terror.

We landed on the roof and the windscreen cracked and shattered as we continued to roll. I tightened my grip around my body and tried to ride it out, but I felt a stinging pain erupt all over.

Then...

Groaning, I lifted my head off the ground, my vision blurring as the world came back into focus. Overhead, the sky was streaked with fire and blood. The sun was setting.

How did I get here?

I could see the car lying beside the highway in the distance. It was a hunk of twisted and broken metal, and behind it was the black car that'd rammed us.

I must've lost consciousness when the car flipped, because I didn't remember being flung out the window at all.

Smoke rose from the twisted wreck, and the engine hissed and clicked in the silence. Where was Chaser? He couldn't be dead. I wouldn't let him die.

My head throbbed and I rolled over with a groan. Red dirt stuck to my arms and coated my T-shirt. Spitting, I cleared the grit from my mouth. Nothing felt broken, but that didn't mean much. Lifting my hand, it was coated with blood and I began to shake.

This was shock, right? *I was going into shock.*

Trembling, I checked my arm. My flesh was shredded—gravel rash—and I almost threw up, but the pain began to fade as I laid there.

I risked another look at the grotesque graze and had to do a double take. My skin was healing, the flesh knitting back together, and then my arm was back to normal as if nothing had ever happened. The wound was gone and my head... All the pain had vanished.

Bloody hell. I'd made the right call turning. It'd just saved my life.

"It's time to give her up, William."

I paused as a gravelly voice echoed across the distance. Raising my head as my faculties returned, I realised I'd been flung a startling distance from the car —about twenty or thirty metres into a ditch but I couldn't be sure. It was far enough that they hadn't found me yet, and I was good with that. I still had a chance.

I couldn't see anyone on the road or in the scrub either, which meant they must be standing on the other side of the wreck.

The gun. I knew Chaser had put it in the glove compartment after things had started to ease between us. He'd trusted me, knowing I was stuck to him—he knew things about werewolves I needed to survive. Did he, though? Did he realise how deep my feelings ran?

Shaking my head, I pushed to my knees and crawled towards the car. He either cared or his humanity was gone. Either way, knowing his true intentions wouldn't help me now.

Crawling towards the car, my gaze darted around, looking for signs of the mystery men. If they were vampires, I'd have to be careful. *Move as silently as possible.* Maybe they'd already smelled the blood, but there was a chance Chaser was bleeding, too—maybe it'd mask my location.

Nothing stirred, so I kept moving, gravel digging into my palms. I'd made it to the road unseen. Through the broken window of the car that'd taken us three-quarters of the way across the country, I spied the glove compartment. It was within reach and all I had to do was...

Two men loomed on the other side of the wreck, and I hesitated.

Chaser was on his knees, his head lowered. An unknown man stood over him and the gun in his hand steadily pointed at Chaser's temple.

My heart twisted, and I forgot all about vampires, werewolves, and my stupid father.

Reaching into the car, I popped open the glove compartment, wincing as the sound echoed. There was a rattle as whatever was inside scraped across plastic.

"I won't ask again," the man said. "Where's the girl?"

"Woman," Chaser replied, his voice rasping. "She's a woman."

"A debt has to be paid, William. If you deny us now, I wonder how long it will take for Fortitude to find out what's really going on here. How long will it be before you die?"

"Not long at all," Chaser declared. "You'll have to shoot me before you take me alive, and you'll have to shoot me before you lay a single finger on her."

Holding my breath, I picked up the gun and pulled my hand back through the broken window.

Checking the magazine, I counted my lucky stars— it was fully loaded—and edged away from the wreck.

How was I going to do this? The man's finger was on the trigger, which meant if I shot at him, he could pull the trigger and kill Chaser. Even if I hit the guy, he could still fire. I saw no other choice.

I had to kill him before...but how? Chaser was on his knees, which meant I had to go for the headshot, or at least the torso. If the man didn't drop on the first shot, I had to be prepared to fire again. No hesitation.

God, help me.

Rising from behind the car, I aimed at the man and fired. A boom echoed across the desert, and I stumbled back as I failed to absorb the kickback through my arm and shoulder.

The man stumbled and clutched his shoulder, turning towards me with a grunt.

I recovered, adrenaline searing through my veins

and stabbing my heart. I fired again, and this time, the bullet found its mark.

It imbedded in his chest, splattering red, and he dropped the gun with a surprised grunt. Falling to his knees, the man's skin withered, his veins bulged, and his entire body turned grey before he fell face-first onto the road.

I'd gotten him in the heart, the wooden bullet putting an end to him.

"Sloane."

I jumped as I felt Chaser's hand curl around mine. He untangled my trembling hand from the gun and clicked the safety on, then he turned me away from the road and the spreading death.

"We have to be careful," I muttered. "There could be more of them."

"There were two," he replied. "I got the other one."

I stared at him, shock setting in. He'd moved so fast, it hadn't even registered.

"Are you okay?" His eyes sparkled in the twilight, and I was almost fooled by the panic I saw in them.

"I was thrown from the car..." I glanced over his shoulder at the outback beyond.

Chaser poked and prodded at me, massaging my arms and ribs, searching for broken bones. When he pressed his palms against my stomach, I shoved him away.

"*Don't.*"

"Sloane, I need to check for broken bones."

"I don't have any."

He grimaced. "It seems the moon follows you even when it sets."

Screw the moon.

"I just killed a man... I just..." I felt his gaze on me, but I couldn't meet it. Killing was second nature to him—he pulled the trigger and had zero regrets—but for me...? "I..."

Chaser stepped forwards and wrapped his arms around me, embracing my body against his. He'd never comforted me. *Never.*

"You saved my life," he whispered into my hair. "No one's ever done that before. No one at all."

CHAPTER 22

CHASER

"What do you mean, no one's ever saved your life?"

I glanced over my shoulder to where Sloane sat beside the road. She was covered in blood, but there weren't any noticeable injuries on her. Her wolf side had done its job and then some.

I was rifling through the black sedan, trying to find anything that'd help, but I wasn't having much luck. Two tyres were blown out, the back axle was cracked, and the fuel tank had a bullet hole in it. Luckily, it hadn't blown the car up.

We weren't driving it anywhere.

I found nothing useful on the bodies, either. The vampires had really upped their faceless men routine.

"Chaser?"

I narrowed my eyes and snatched the tyre iron out

of the boot. Sloane was covered in her own blood and the smell was tugging at my composure.

"Aren't you worried another car will find us?" she asked, changing tactics. "If someone finds us with those bodies, we're screwed."

Striding over to the twisted wreck that used to be my car, I shoved the end of the tyre iron under the lip of the boot and heaved. Metal groaned, then gave way as it opened. Our bags tumbled out and collided with the road, the sound of something smashing caused Sloane to scramble to her feet.

"That better not be my laptop," she exclaimed.

I tossed Sloane her bag, which landed at her feet with a thud.

"If you've got a jumper in there, you'd better put it on," I commanded. "It gets cold out here at night."

She rifled through her bag, wailing when she saw her laptop's shattered screen. I narrowed my eyes but said nothing. This was her way of coping after she'd killed that vampire. It wasn't easy killing, and even though Sloane was one tough woman, nothing was more confronting than taking a life, human *or* supernatural.

Watching her take out a cardigan, I picked up my bag and slung it over my shoulder, making sure the gun I'd taken from the heavies was tucked into the waistband of my jeans. When Sloane stood, I handed her back her gun.

"I..." she began, staring at my outstretched hand.

"Take it," I said. "You wanted it a week ago, so here it is."

"I don't think..."

"You could've shot me," I told her. "But you didn't."

She pursed her lips and stared at the gun. After a moment, she reached out and took it.

"It's a hard thing," I murmured. "The first time."

"Hopefully, it was the last," she muttered before setting out down the road.

Watching her walk away from the wreck and the bodies, I sighed. I knew it was only the first of many, but it would only harm her if I told her the truth. Being a werewolf or a supernatural was challenging enough, but a wolf who could turn at will...? It would be survival of the fittest for the rest of her life.

"If I didn't feel like throwing up, I might like it out here," Sloane declared, her voice loud in the silence.

"Are you feeling sick?" I asked, catching up to her.

Stopping, I grasped her arm. She didn't fight me when I placed my palm against her forehead. She was a little warm.

"It's nothing."

"You feel warm."

"If I were going to die from internal bleeding, I'd already be dead," she stated. "My wolfness healed me. It's fine."

"You killed him to survive. He would've come after you once he killed me."

She glanced up at the sky. "I know."

A melancholy howl echoed across the vast landscape, and she stiffened.

"What's that?" she asked, her head twisting towards the noise.

"Calm down, it's just a dingo. The full moon is long gone."

She shivered and looked around at the landscape.

"Keep walking," I commanded. "The sooner we find civilisation, the sooner we're back on the road."

There was no reply, and we walked in silence as the sun went down.

"He called you William," she said after a while. "Why?"

Sloane could never leave things unsaid for too long. How much had she heard before she shot that guy? Best to play it by ear and not give too much away. My past wasn't her business or burden to carry. She had enough of her own problems to worry about.

"Because that's my name," I said after a pause.

"Your real name?"

"You think my parents called me Chaser?" I asked, raising my eyebrow.

"*No.*"

She stopped walking, and I turned, peering at her in the darkness. Her long hair was tangled and strewn with dirt, the knees of her jeans were ripped open, the toes of her boots were scuffed, but she was still beautiful. The sight of her tore my dead heart in two.

"What?" I snapped.

"You don't like talking very much."

I rolled my eyes. "What gave it away?"

"I still want to run away with you, you know."

I grunted and started walking. A moment later, the sound of her footsteps caught up to me.

"Do you think they were watching us back at the lake?" she asked.

"Possibly."

She shivered. "Are we going to sleep out here?"

I glanced up at the sliver of moon and shrugged. "Maybe."

"But we've got nothing to make a fire, and there are dingoes out there..." As if on cue, another howl echoed through the night. "Are they..."

"Are they what?"

"Attracted to..." she gestured to herself, "*werewolves*."

I snorted. "It's about ten kilometres to the nearest town," I said. "That's about five hours in werewolf speed." A smirk pulled at my mouth. "Or I could just carry you."

She screwed up her face. "You want to carry me?"

"Yes." I pointed to the sign that was looming out in the darkening twilight. "Five hours or forty-five minutes, take your pick."

Sloane scowled, which only caused me to laugh.

"Don't laugh at me," she complained. "Five-hour walk? Stuff that. *Carry me*."

Sighing, I turned and tapped my shoulder. "Put your bag on your back and get on."

I waited as Sloane fumbled with her duffel, then her warm hands were on my shoulders. She leapt up and wrapped her arms around my neck, and I grasped her knees.

"Don't let go," I warned, then I turned away from the last smear of sunlight on the horizon, and I ran.

Forever moving east... Straight into the lion's den.

I slowed to a walk when we reached the first signs of civilisation.

The lights were on at the local pub, the street outside clogged with cars and utes, and music and noise echoed through the open windows.

Sloane wriggled on my back, and I loosened my grip. She landed on the road, her boots thudding on the asphalt. The scent of her blood began to dissipate but it still hung around me like an intoxicating perfume.

"I think I've got wind burn," she complained.

Ignoring her, I held my breath and scanned the street.

There wasn't much to this town other than the pub. A post office, a small supermarket, a couple of boarded-up shops that looked as if they harkened back to a time I barely remembered, and a house or two in the distance.

Spying a car parked farther down the road, away from the lights of the pub, I crossed to the opposite side of the road and kept to the shadows.

Sloane followed, mirroring my steps.

The car was an old beat-up Holden, a late 90s model, which was good for us. New cars were difficult to hot-wire with their advanced computer systems and immobilisers. I didn't have time to mingle at the pub and compel a set of keys from a local. The less faces that saw us, the better.

I tried the driver's side door and found it unlocked. Ducking inside, I leaned underneath the dash and began to pull at the wiring.

Sloane leaned against the car and watched me, her eyes burning a hole into my back.

"You really know a lot of stuff, don't you?"

I grunted as I stripped the wiring.

"Do you know how to whittle?"

"I'm a vampire, not Crocodile Dundee," I drawled, sparking the wires. The engine turned over and I slipped into the seat, tossing my bag into the back. "Get in."

She ducked around to the other side and got in the front, easing her bag on her lap.

I backed the car up, leaving the headlights off, and turned down a side street, taking us into the bush.

When I was satisfied that we were far enough from town, I pulled over.

"What are you doing?" Sloane asked, her eyes on me.

"You need to change your clothes," I commanded, getting out of the car. We were both filthy from the accident. Blood stained the front of my T-shirt, and Sloane was covered in it—and I was tired of holding my breath.

She didn't argue as she stepped out onto the dark road. Taking out a clean T-shirt and a pair of jeans, she stripped out of her clothes. "Where are we going now?"

"We're going to Adelaide." I turned my back to give her some privacy. "Then we're dumping the car and getting a train."

"A train? Seriously?"

"They won't expect it."

She snorted. "You've got that right. Australia isn't exactly the train capital of the world."

Opening the back, I grabbed my bag and found some clean clothes. I took off my bloodied T-shirt and jeans. As I was pulling on a fresh pair of trousers, I sensed Sloane staring.

I knew I intrigued her, but I wasn't sure if it was her newly-awakened wolf instincts or her desperation to understand the world she now found herself in. I wasn't any good for her, even if I was free to choose.

Lifting my head, I caught her gaze over the roof of the car. Her chin lowered as her heart skipped, and I narrowed my eyes as my humanity stirred. It was growing a little every day, creeping back in like a bad smell that just wouldn't quit.

Glad the car was between us, I pulled on a clean T-shirt and stashed the dirty one back in my bag.

"If you're done, get back in the car," I snapped. "The sooner we get into the city, the better."

Sloane sighed and wrenched the back door open, threw her bag in, and slammed it closed. The sound echoed down the lonely road, and I got back in the front. I sparked the wires again and the engine turned over.

Sloane got back in, her gaze hard. "Chaser, for once—"

"I know what you want," I interrupted, putting on my seat belt. "But I'm not the comforting type."

She stared at me as I pressed my foot on the accelerator. The wheels spun in the gravel and we took off the moment we hit asphalt.

"Yeah, right," she muttered, knowing I could hear. *"Pull the other one."*

CHAPTER 23
SLOANE

I'd never been to Adelaide before. I stared out the window, taking everything in, as we drove our stolen Holden through the centre of the city. The parks, the churches, the treelined streets...all of it. If we weren't on the run, I would've loved to stay a while.

The city was barely awake as we dumped the car on a back street. Keeping our heads down, we made our way to the train station. It sat on the edge of the central business district, flanked by wide-open green spaces, making it feel as if we were back in the bush.

Chaser organised tickets, using his fancy vampire mind control, while I waited near the platform.

I watched him flirt with the female cashier and scowled. After everything we'd been through, after hearing his real name, I was understanding just how much I didn't know—about Chaser, about werewolves, about Fortitude. Nothing had changed, even after I'd killed that vampire. I'd turned, but I still didn't understand what it meant.

I knew how I felt, but I couldn't reconcile the two parts of myself. Add Chaser into the mix, and I had a whole truckload of problems.

He turned from the counter and sauntered over to me.

"There's an Overland train leaving this morning," he said, slipping the tickets into his bag. "It will take us all the way to Melbourne."

"How convenient," I drawled.

"I can see your attitude is back."

"I'm wondering how I'd fare jumping from a moving train," I went on, my anger rising. "I did survive a car crash."

"And how do you think you'd fare with two broken legs?" Chaser asked. "How long do you think they'd take to heal? If they heal at all."

A sob threatened to escape, and I sank down onto the bench behind me, hiding my face from him.

"What? Giving up so soon?"

Chaser's renewed coldness felt like a knife in my heart, and I almost wished I'd kept running the night I'd turned.

"Sloane." He sat beside me.

"Just stop, Chaser," I snapped. "I'm sick of all this emotional whiplash. Either you care or you don't. I've got bigger things to worry about."

"Bigger things than what?"

"That's the million-dollar question," I said. "I know there's things you're not telling me. Things about what I am and why those vampires want me...and the real reason my father wants to control me. I have a right to know."

"Maybe, but it's not for me—"

"Yeah, yeah, *I know*." Exhaustion was driving my irritation as my fate closed around me. The light was fading, and possible escape routes were being shut off one by one. Once we get on that train, it'll almost be over. "Who are you, Chaser? More importantly, who are you to me? *The mystery deepens*."

"We don't have time for this," he said as the train approached the station. Passengers began to gathering their things and a whistle blew.

"We never have time when things get too hard, Chaser. Don't worry, I know how men like you operate."

"Unlikely."

I snorted, not wanting to argue about the fact that I felt like I was stuck between some suspected unrequited love and a father whose motives were even more mysterious than the Bermuda Triangle.

The game was changing so fast, I could hardly keep up.

He wouldn't let anything happen to me? How was it only now that I realised it was a promise he couldn't keep?

Chaser snorted and picked up our bags as the train

eased alongside the platform. "Contrary to popular belief, I do care about you, Sloane. The only person standing between you and your belief of that is you."

Rolling my eyes, I climbed onto the train behind him, thoroughly annoyed he'd gotten in the last word. *Again.*

Deep down, I knew Chaser cared about me. I saw it in the way he made sure I was never hungry, how I'd always gotten the bed and the first shower, how he took a bullet for me, how he trusted me when he gave me my gun back, and when he'd agreed to let me turn. I didn't know why he held himself back from giving more than that—maybe it *was* merely duty that stood in his way—but I knew exactly what kept me from saying the words out loud.

Chaser was one of *them*; he was Fortitude, and I was afraid he'd turn out to be nothing more than a disciple of violence and brutality like the rest of them. So, I didn't tell him.

He didn't want to run away with me, and he didn't want to help me escape my father. Maybe if I told myself that, then it would be easier when we parted ways.

Maybe my heart wouldn't break when he walked away.

Maybe I'd be able to survive the storm to come if I wasn't completely shattered.

Maybe...

Staring out the window, I watched the platform move away from us, and the city flashed past as the train picked up speed. The central part of town morphed into an industrial zone, and then the factories melted away into wilderness. Overhead, the sky was blue, and below, the earth was scorched.

The train was more modern than I'd expected. We had a little private room with a shower and toilet, but when I said little, I meant shoebox-sized.

There was a seat with reclining sections and a separate chair. At night, the seat somehow converted to a bed, and above it was a fold-down bunk. Ten or so smaller compartments made up the bulk of the carriage, along with other cars that held standard seating, fancier suites, a restaurant, and more.

Everything was grey and red, which reflected my mood perfectly.

"You want a shower?" Chaser asked.

I nodded and peered into the tight space, making a face. The shower was so small, it sat over the toilet. It would have to do. I smelled and felt like a giant wad of stinky trash. Plus, my hair was still full of grit, grime, and dried blood from the accident.

"Turn around," I said, glaring at him.

Chaser grunted, angled his body away from me, and stared out the window.

Stripping, I left my dirty clothes on the seat and

closed myself inside the cubicle. Dousing myself with warm water, I tried not to focus on the last twenty-four hours and allowed my thoughts to wander.

I scrubbed off the filth of our car crash drama as best I could with the little square of soap provided.

The image of the world tumbling around and around filled my mind, and I pressed my palm against the wall to steady myself. It didn't help that the train was moving, and I breathed deeply. Calmness only made my ears ring with the sound of the fatal gunshot...and the withered corpse on the side of the road.

That vampire was a bad guy. He deserved it. It was him or me...*him or Chaser*. I didn't even know who they were.

Forcing myself to squash the memories, I washed the suds out of my hair and smoothed through some conditioner. As I rinsed, I made plans so I would have something else to focus on.

Within a day or two, Chaser and I would arrive at the Fortitude compound, and our whirlwind road trip would be over. Chaser, *William*, star employee of the Fortitude wolves, branded lackey to my father... Time was limited if I wanted to solve the one mystery that would haunt me for the rest of my miserable days. Who was the vampire I'd grown to care about? Who was the *man* underneath the blood and fangs?

My heart twisted at the thought of him. Too many emotional responses in such a short amount of time had me overloaded. I was spiralling into a one-way ticket to a psych ward.

I had to stop caring.

I'd killed a man to save him.

This was my last chance to convince Chaser to either let me go or come with me. I could tell him how I felt now or forever hold my peace and die a slow, miserable death at the hands of Fortitude.

Emerging from the little cubicle, I pulled on my clothes, bumping against Chaser as the train moved from side to side. The accidental touch made my heart twist, and I scowled. I hated that he'd heard it.

Sitting in the seat closest to the window, I towel-dried my hair and watched as he rifled through his stuff, taking out a T-shirt and a pair of dark-coloured jeans and boxers. I wrinkled my nose when he sniffed the T-shirt, checking for freshness or blood, I wasn't sure which.

He didn't speak as he closed himself inside the cubicle. Turning my head, I realised his bag was still lying open on the seat next to me, his belongings on show. Inside, I could see his wallet, gun, spare ammo, and my Ziplock bag of money. All the things I wanted to steal from him way back at the beginning of our messed-up road trip. They were just lying there, ripe for the picking.

Glancing at the door, I knew only a handful of inches separated me from Chaser. It made the thought of rifling through his things even more exhilarating.

Reaching out, I picked up his wallet and ran my fingers over the soft leather square. After all we'd been through, he finally trusted me, which made what I was about to do all the more terrible. I could've trusted him in return and told him how I felt, but there were just too many secrets he was holding back.

So, I opened his wallet.

Inside were a few twenty-dollar notes and the usual bits and pieces. There was a credit card with the name William Mason and a matching Victorian driver's license. Tilting the card back and forth, I studied the photo. It wasn't half bad, the lucky bastard. The address and date of birth were fake, so I didn't pay too much attention to that. It was starting to bother me that I didn't know Chaser's real name until now. It felt like he'd been touting a lie this entire time, but did I have any right to be angry about it? I knew what he was and despite that, I fell for him anyway.

Checking his wallet again, a piece of paper tucked into one of the card slots caught my eye, and I pulled it out. Turning it over, I froze.

It was an old-fashioned sepia photograph of a woman, like one of those studio portraits. She had long dark hair with a feathered fascinator pinned to the side, pale skin, and big eyes, her black and cream lace dress buttoned up to her neck. She couldn't be a day over twenty-five—the same age as me. There was this sweet and wholesome look about her that didn't fit Chaser at all.

Who was she? She was obviously someone special to him; otherwise, why would he carry her picture everywhere? A picture he'd probably been carrying for a hundred and thirty years.

I scowled as jealousy burned in my gut. Maybe she was the reason things had never quite changed between us, why he didn't want to help me. I didn't like her, whoever she was.

The bathroom door opened, and I jumped, my heart skipping a beat. Chaser's gaze fell to the wallet in my lap and then to the photograph in my hands. His demeanour changed in an instant.

"Get a good look?" he snarled.

I swallowed hard and held up the photo. "Who is she?"

Chaser's expression was pure anger, and for a split-second, I faltered. Then he said the last thing I was expecting. "She's my wife."

Everything fell away, and my hands trembled, the photograph shaking. It was as if my body was tearing apart, my heart barely holding on. The world shook, and the foundations of everything I believed in had shattered. Destruction only took a second after all.

His...*wife?* My gaze fell to his hand. He didn't wear a ring, and there wasn't a mark... There wouldn't be, though, would there? He was a vampire. I'd be a fool to think he hadn't had several lifetimes of relationships, but he spoke about her as if she were still alive.

At the beginning of our road trip nightmare,

Chaser and I sat at that roadhouse pub and argued about trust and death. I'd found no one I would die for—not until I'd shot that vampire by the side of the road before he could kill Chaser—not until his life was on the line.

In that moment, I knew I would die for him because that was what you did for those you cared about. I just didn't understand it until now.

"You did," I whispered. "You found someone you'd die for." *And it wasn't me.* It was the most selfish thing I could've thought at that moment, but it hurt. I'd always been the package he was ordered to deliver to Fortitude.

I was no one.

"You were never going to help me, were you?" I asked, my voice trembling.

"I can't."

"*Why?*"

He snatched the photo out of my hands and shoved it into his pocket.

His silence only drove another hot poker into my heart, and I glanced away before he could see my welling tears.

"I told you about me and Fortitude," he went on, his voice thin. "I'm indebted to them. They—"

"I don't need to hear it," I snapped.

"You do."

"You're dead to me." I seethed. "*Dead.*"

"That's what happened to her," he said, sitting beside me.

"*Stop it.*" I leaned my forehead against the window, the cool glass numbing my skin.

Chaser growled and grasped my arm. Wrenching me towards him, I let out a cry as I hit his chest. His gaze caught mine and wouldn't let go.

"*Let me go.*"

"Those vampires who are after you," he continued, his expression pure thunder, "are the same vampires who took her from me. History will not repeat itself, Sloane. You hear me? *I won't let it.*"

I froze, trying to make sense of this whole mess. His wife had been murdered by the same vampires who were trying to kill me. Was that why he cared? I was his redemption? His second chance? This had nothing to do with *caring* and had everything to do with his own selfish closure.

I was a pawn, always had been.

"I made a deal with Fortitude," he said. "They help me get revenge, and in exchange, they—"

"*I don't care.*" I shook my head and felt a black hole of sadness open inside me.

He didn't reply; he stared at me, his forehead creasing.

"I should never have let you in," I snarled, wrenching out of his grasp. He looked as if he'd been slapped, and it only made my rage intensify. I turned away from him, focusing on the landscape rushing past the window. "You're just like all the others. You're just like my father. Small, manipulative, sadistic, and power hungry. *I killed a man for you.*"

"*Sloane.*"

I felt his hand on my shoulder, and I shook him off with a violent jerk. "*Don't touch me.*"

"No, you don't understand."

"You don't get to command me," I said with a snarl, rising to my feet. "I am not yours! I don't belong to you, Chaser."

"*Sloane.*" He stood before me. "You don't understand."

"I'm such a fool..." I murmured, my gaze searching his. "*Never again.*"

It was a promise, a threat, a contract written in blood.

Never. Again.

CHAPTER 24
SLOANE

I was back at square one.

Chaser was my kidnapper, and I was nothing but cargo. Which only meant one thing...

I had to get away from him before we reached Melbourne because by then, it would be too late to do anything. This train and one of the few stops along the line was my only chance.

I'd curled up in the corner of the seat by the window to put as much distance between us as I could. The size of the room wasn't helping. Chaser sat opposite, his gaze stuck on me like superglue.

I was doing my best to ignore him, but I squirmed, my heartbeat annoyingly irregular.

Finally, his incessant staring got the better of me.

"Don't look at me," I snapped, throwing the first thing my hand fell on.

The mobile phone smacked him in the chest, and

he smirked as he put it back into his bag on the seat beside me. He leaned close, making a point of brushing against my leg.

"Don't touch me, either."

"Don't lie to me, Sloane," he murmured, kneeling before me.

"Oh, that's rich coming from you."

"I never owed you anything." His palms came to rest on my knees.

We stared at one another, a million insults rolling around in my mind.

"I'm hungry," I said, blurting out something before I punched him in the face. A few hours ago, I would've thought about risking my life to kiss him, but now that urge had faded into nothing.

"I'll go to the dining car," he said, rising to his feet. "Don't let anyone else in."

I narrowed my eyes and turned my attention out the window to the bush rolling past.

He grunted, then opened the door and a moment later, it slammed closed.

The tiny room became a lot larger in his absence, and I breathed deeply. It was the first time I'd been truly alone since he'd taken me away, and it was an exhilarating feeling.

Sitting up, I went for his bag. Unzipping the black leather duffle, I took out my money and the extra ammo. His gun wasn't there, apparently, he'd taken it with him.

Grabbing my bag, I tipped out the contents and discarded anything I didn't need. I dumped my laptop, the mobile phone, and half my toiletries and clothes. Packing away my money and ammo, I shouldered the bag and opened the door.

Peering out into the narrow hallway, I found it was empty.

I had no idea how far it was until the next stop, but I wouldn't have another chance. I'd have to risk breaking my legs and hoping they'd still heal without the power of the full moon.

Movement caught my eye, and I jumped. Seeing it was only a conductor, I straightened and stepped into the hallway. The man smiled when he saw me, and it put my fluttering heart at ease.

"Excuse me," I called out, "where's the café car?"

"Six cars to your right," the man said with a nod.

I smiled and darted down the corridor to the left. Chaser was a master at hunting people down—or so he said—so this time, I had to be better at hiding my tracks.

At the end of the carriage there was a toilet and a large luggage storage area packed full of suitcases and bags, and a door leading to the next car. I glanced over my shoulder, but the conductor was gone.

I pushed through to the next carriage, which looked exactly the same as the one I'd been in.

The train lurched, making me stumble. I caught myself at the last second, my fingers grasping the railing. My bag fell to the ground with a thud, and I cursed.

"Whoa there," a voice said. Hands clamped on my shoulders, and I instinctively jerked away.

Raising my head, I gasped and fell back against the wall, the railing pressing into the small of my back. Black eyes stared back at me and a coldness spread through my skin.

Vampire.

"We've been looking for you," the man snarled. "You shouldn't have run."

My heart skipped a beat and I twisted away, attempting to run back the way I came.

The vampire grabbed my arm and pulled hard. I fell, smashing my jaw on the railing as he dragged me back.

I opened my mouth to scream, but his hand clamped over my face as the other twisted in my hair. He dragged me up and held me against his body.

"Don't struggle," the vampire rasped, pressing his mouth against my neck. "I just want a little taste."

"Let her go," an unfamiliar voice drawled.

A surge of hope flared inside me, and I struggled against the vampire's hold. Searching for the source of the mysterious stranger, my gaze met a pair of cold, black eyes.

The conductor.

In that moment I knew. *This was a trap.*

The second vampire smirked, then nodded down the corridor.

"Get her inside," he said. "I won't ask again, Bailey."

I screamed as I realised I was screwed, but the sound was muffled. No one was going to hear me. No one at all.

Bailey hauled me to my feet, cursing under his breath as he dragged me down the narrow hall and into a room at the end.

It was much larger than the compartment Chaser and I had, but I wasn't interested in the décor. Once I'd been hauled inside, the conductor closed the door and flipped the lock. My bag was in his hands, and my gaze followed it.

Bailey let me go, shoving me roughly into the seat. Fear and a mixture of bile rose in the back of my throat, and it was all I could do to stop terror from overpowering me. If there was a way to fight back, then I had to.

When Chaser came back from the dining car, he would see I was gone and come looking. Wouldn't he?

My gaze flickered to the door.

"What does he call himself these days?" the conductor asked, his lips curving into an evil smile. "Chaser?"

"Stupid name, if you ask me," Bailey said.

"I wasn't asking you," the other vampire snapped.

"You know Chaser?" I muttered. Of course, they

did. The vampires who'd rammed us off the road knew him by name, too.

"He got what was coming to him," Bailey said with a smirk. "Eye for an eye."

I went to stand, my lip curling in a snarl, but the conductor pushed me back down.

"There's no getting out of this, Betty," he said calmly. "Fortitude crossed us, William screwed us over, and now we have to take payment. It's nothing personal." He eyed me, his gaze raking over my body, taking in every bump and curve. "We're not the kind of men who show mercy. Mercy is not in our vocabulary. Violence, pain, blood, death, murder... Those are words we understand."

I tensed, my throat constricting. Why weren't they finishing me off? Why weren't they putting a bullet into my head and throwing my limp body off the train? Chaser wasn't coming—they'd made that much clear. Which meant...

Chaser was dead.

I swallowed a wail of despair. What was the point? There was no way out...there was nothing left.

"Just end it," I managed to croak out.

The conductor smirked. "You think we want to kill you? What has William been telling you, little wolf?" He shook his head as Bailey laughed. "You're more valuable to us alive, but after we're through with you, you'll likely wish you were dead."

"I'll kill you," I hissed, seething. "I'll ram a stake right through your heart."

The vampire snorted and raised his eyebrows. "Hear that? That sounds like a party."

"She's got fight in her," Bailey leered. "I like it when they struggle."

I tensed. *"You'll never win."*

The conductor's hand grasped my face and forced me to look at him.

"Oh, but little wolf...*we already have.*"

CHAPTER 25

CHASER

I closed the door behind me and gritted my teeth.

Sloane was never meant to find out anything. About her werewolf side, about me being a vampire, about Fortitude...about that photograph. I was meant to deliver her to her father as promised, then things would go back to the way they were before I left Melbourne. At least, they were supposed to.

I hadn't bargained on a lot of things in my life, least of all meeting Sloane.

A cough drew my attention, breaking me out of my spiralling thoughts. My gaze slammed into a familiar face, and I growled. Ginger-coloured hair, poor choice in clothing, ratty beard, and black eyes full of murder —the vampire from behind the *Sailor's Arms*.

He was standing at the end of the corridor, smiling at me in triumph. I pulled my gun and took a purposeful step towards him.

Sensing my reaction, the vampire retreated into the next carriage, and I followed.

Sloane would be fine as long as she stayed put like I told her. Kept the door locked. Tried nothing stupid. There was nowhere for her to go on a moving train.

Leaning against the wall, I eased open the door and listened. The sound of the wheels grinding on the metal tracks drowned out everything. I'd have to go in blind.

Rage burned through my veins as I pushed through the door, my shoulder banging against the wall as the train swayed. The moment I was off-balance, a hand shot out and grasped my wrist, slamming it to the side.

I grunted as the vampire collided with me, his elbow striking me in the temple. I shoved him away and my grip loosened on the gun. He wrenched my wrist as he stumbled backwards, twisting until my fingers loosened, and the firearm clattered to the floor.

We eyed each other for a long second, then he pulled a knife from his pocket and held it out in front of him. My gaze flickered to the gun between us. The wooden bullets would be an advantage, but I could rip him apart with my bare hands if I had to.

I had to put an end to him before he got me, otherwise, Sloane was done for.

The vampire lunged and the knife came with him. Metal flashed, and I flung my body to the side, but there was nowhere to go. I grunted in pain as steel stabbed into my thigh, embedding into my flesh, and I fell back against the wall.

He was on me in a flash, his strength almost overwhelming me. He must be older than me—the more age a vampire had, the stronger they were. His fist smashed into my head and stars burst through my vision, exploding like iridescent fireworks.

Stunned, I reached for the gun, but the vampire kicked it away as he strode towards me. Leaning over my stunned body, he grabbed my hair, his expression contorting.

"Eye for an eye, William. How does it feel?"

He slammed my head against the wall, and the world blurred. When he ripped out the knife, I hissed, not giving him the pleasure of hearing me howl in pain. And when he shoved me onto my side and smashed my head into the ground, I knew I was a goner.

They knew we were here.

And I'd been lured into their trap.

I shouldn't have spoken to her like that, I thought as my thigh burned and my head swirled. *Now she's on her own.*

She's alone, and she hates me. She thinks...

My head collided with the floor again, and as the world faded, I saw the vampire aim the gun at my heart.

"Darling…"

I stirred, my eyes taking their sweet time adjusting to the brightness.

"William, are you all right?"

I blinked, dazed. The sun shone overhead, and the air was full of the salty tang of the ocean. Focusing on the woman in front of me, my limbs went numb.

"Loretta?"

The wind tossed her chestnut hair around and a strand caught on her pink lips. She swiped it away and laughed, the sound pulling at my heart.

"You've had too much sun," she said. "Just one more minute, and we'll go back, I promise."

"Where am I?" I murmured. Running my hands over my chest, I looked for a wound.

We were standing on a bluff overlooking the ocean. I could see white chalk cliffs in the distance, hear the crash of the waves below, and feel the sun on my shoulders. I remembered this day—the last we'd had together by the cliffs of Dover on the coast of England.

I also remembered being on a train with Sloane in Australia well over a century later.

"It's okay," Loretta said. "It's been a long time."

She rose to her feet and walked towards me, her eyes full of an understanding I didn't recognise. Her fingers closed around mine.

"A picture won't fill the hole in your heart," she whispered, the wind tugging her words.

"What did you say?" I asked with a frown.

Her gaze met mine. "She needs you, William."

"Who?"

Loretta smiled, her hands cupping my face. "It's okay to let me go. It's okay to love again."

"But..."

The light dimmed around us and I shivered, my chest throbbing with a hot pain. My knee buckled, but I didn't fall. My gaze was caught on Loretta's, and she held me upright.

"One hundred years..." I whispered.

She nodded. "It's time, don't you think?"

"I..."

My vision blurred, and I groaned, my head lolling from side to side. Blinking, the haze cleared. I was surrounded by empty luggage racks and a trail of my blood smeared across the floor.

The ground moved beneath me, the sound of wheels clicking over tracks bringing clarity back. I lifted my head with a groan as life began to move through my withered veins. I'd desiccated, the wooden bullet tearing through my heart...but I was still alive.

Hauling myself up, my head spun and my entire body felt clammy. *The talisman.* I rubbed my hand against my healed chest, the brand tingling with fading magic.

Not even death could free me. Forever a slave.

No time for self-pity, I thought with a grimace. *I have to get to Sloane. I have to find her...*

The train car was empty outside the luggage compartment.

Dragging myself down the corridor, I stumbled into the next carriage and back to our compartment. Wrenching the door open, I frowned when I saw our stuff strewn all over the seat and floor. Immediately, I knew Sloane had run, which could only mean...

They had her.

I opened the door and scanned the hallway. I had to find her before we reached the next station or she'd be gone forever.

Glancing to the right, I knew she wouldn't have gone that way—that was the way she thought I'd went. Turning left, I limped down the hall and into the next car, my withered body crying out for blood.

When I found that ginger vampire and his mates, they were going to wish they'd never been born. I'd drain them dry and make them *beg*.

I'd unleash the monster within. *The monster they'd created.*

CHAPTER 26

SLOANE

C *haser was dead.*

The realisation burned through me, tearing everything apart. My heart, my mind, my body, my soul... That was how I knew my feelings weren't a passing fancy. I wouldn't be able to forget him, no matter what I did. If he'd dumped me at Fortitude and ridden off into the sunset, I would've pined after him for the rest of my life like a stupid little girl.

Chaser was a part of me now, whether I wanted him or not.

"Why don't you just kill me?" I asked, my voice sounding almost robotic to my ears. "Just end it."

The conductor snorted. "You'll love being a blood slave, Betty. We've got grand plans for you. The sacrifice will go ahead and once it does, no one will be able to stand against us."

I stared numbly out the window, my entire body

feeling listless in my despair.

I should've done something. Fought back, tried to end it, but everything was just out of reach. My fingertips scraped the edges of caring about my fate, but I couldn't quite grasp it.

Chaser was dead.

I shouldn't have said those things to him. I was angry. Upset. He had a life before me. Of course, he did. So had I.

"She's giving up," the conductor mused. "Can you see it in her eyes?"

Bailey leaned over me and stared into my face. His breath stank like rancid meat, and I growled, kneeing him as hard as I could in the balls. He doubled over with a cry, grasping his crotch as the other vampire laughed.

Bailey let out a cry of rage and fisted my hair. "You'll never escape. This is your life, *wolf*. A glorified blood bag. That's all it'll ever be."

"We'll see about that," I drawled. "*I know what I am.*"

"*You're lying.*"

Bailey raised his hand, but before he could hit me, the door slid open, and I gasped as my gaze collided with Chaser.

The conductor pulled a gun with a snarl, and I cried out, but Chaser was too fast. He slammed the heel of his palm against the vampire's wrist, forcing the gun to the side as it went off.

The boom was deafening in the small space, and my ears rang as the two vampires wrestled.

Bailey lunged, desperate to join in the fray, but I was on him in a flash. I kicked his knee out from under him, forcing him to buckle to the floor with an angry grunt.

I threw myself on him and fisted my hands in his greasy, ginger hair. Slamming his face into the floor, I let out an enraged cry, the wolf within awakening with a lust for violence I'd never felt before.

Strength surged through my veins and I growled, succumbing to the wildness within.

"Bitch!" Bailey howled. "You turned. *You turned!*"

We were squashed in the room like sardines in a tin, but I was hardly aware of what Chaser was doing. The gun hadn't gone off again and there was still movement around me as I tried to bash Bailey's face in.

The vampire bucked underneath me, and the force dislodged my grasp. I fell back against the seat and thrashed as his hands closed around my neck.

"*Choke, little wolf,*" he snarled through a mouthful of blood. "*Your pack won't save you now.*"

I clawed at him, desperate to finish the job as I gasped for air. *Not today. Not like this.*

A body fell to the floor beside me, and I kicked, thrashing against Bailey's hold. Then Chaser was standing over us.

Without a single shred of hesitation, he rammed a bloodstained hand through Bailey's back and kicked him to the side, ripping his heart clean from his chest. Instantly, the hands around my neck slackened, and I gasped, coughing as air rushed into my starving lungs.

Grabbing me underneath the arms, Chaser hauled me out of the room and into the hall, away from the blood.

It was all over in a matter of minutes, and I stared at Chaser with something close to awe. I'd seen him in action before, but this was something else. He was a whirlwind of death, precise and brutal. *A shadow…*

My eyes filled with tears. "I thought you were dead."

"I was," he replied, his grip loosening. He stepped away from me, limping heavily.

"What do you mean?" I asked. "You don't mean literally, do you? *Do you?*"

He didn't reply, which was his typical response when he didn't feel like explaining anything.

"Help me," he said after a moment, reaching down and grasping the conductor's wrists. He dragged the body down the hall, having some difficulty.

"What are you doing? What if—"

"These cars are empty," he said. "No one will see us. It was a trap from the start."

I lowered my gaze, trying not to look at the bodies on the floor.

"Give me a hand."

I grimaced and lifted the first vampire by the

ankles. He was all grey and withered...but he was still warm.

We leaned him in the alcove by the outer door, and then went back for what was left of Bailey. My stomach rolled as I caught the gaze of their empty eyes.

Chaser wiped his bloodied hands on the dead vampire's clothes, then forced the outer door open. I grasped the handrail as wind whipped through my hair. The ground was rushing past at a terrifying speed, and it'd only take one stumble in the wrong direction to fall. One little misstep, and I would be dragged underneath the train and onto the tracks.

I glanced at Chaser and nodded when his gaze met mine. I was ready.

Together, we lifted what was left of the vampires and rolled them out the door. As their bodies hit the ground, the sound of their flesh being torn apart by the train made me wince.

I turned away, and the noise was cut off as Chaser heaved the door back into place.

"Why isn't the train stopping?" I asked. "Surely there's an emergency procedure..."

"Let's get our stuff," he said, ignoring my question. "The next station is only minutes away. We need to be gone before they find what we left behind."

Picking up my bag, I followed him up the stairs, not liking the way he limped. I could see the pain he was doing his damnedest to ignore.

"Chaser?" I asked as we moved down the hall and

back into our carriage.

He grunted as he opened the door to our compartment.

"Are you sure you're all right? You said... You said you were dead."

"I need blood," he replied. "But we don't have time."

"But—"

"Sloane, *please*."

I tensed, my questions dying before they reached my lips, and I nodded.

Scooping up my things, I shoved them into my duffel as the landscape outside filled with power lines and buildings—the station was almost upon us.

When we were done, we moved down the corridor and waited by the outer door of the carriage. My skin prickled in anticipation as the train rolled into the station. Chaser looked unnaturally grey, his veins bulging a little too much. He was a borderline mummy.

"How do we do this?" I asked, staring fretfully at the platform. "Are you strong enough to do your mind trick thing?"

"Compulsion," he corrected. "And no, we're gong to have to do this the old-fashioned way."

I grimaced. "Run?"

"Put your head down and walk," Chaser told me. "Act natural and don't panic."

"Sounds easy when you say it like that."

"Follow my lead and we'll slip right out of here."

I hoped he was right.

The train finally came to a stop, the brakes screeching. The moment the doors disengaged, I forced it open and we stepped out onto the platform. Chaser winced, but he never made a sound.

Putting my head down, I linked my arm through his, and we walked down the platform with the other disembarking passengers. I startled as a group of uniformed men from the train walked toward us, but they passed without looking twice.

"Keep walking," Chaser murmured as a commotion broke out behind us.

Swallowing hard, I resisted the urge to look back. People around us were already stopping to see what all the fuss was about, but we kept moving.

We turned into the main building, passing noticeboards and waiting areas. Our footsteps were muffled by the commotion of passengers coming and going. Loved ones embraced, taxi drivers loaded luggage into the boots of their cars, people rolled suitcases towards a bus stop, and we melted into the scenery.

Exiting the building, we walked down the street, disappearing into the wilds of the little town of nowhere, Victoria.

No one called out or chased us down.

No one tried to stop us.

No one at all.

CHAPTER 27

SLOANE

Bringing the car to a stop, I rolled down the window and looked for Chaser.

I didn't see him at first and my heart twisted in my chest, but then he emerged out of the shadows like a ghost. He was exactly where I'd left him half an hour ago when I'd gone off to find us a more reliable means of transportation.

He slid into the front passenger seat, dumping his bag at his feet. Once he'd shut the door and clipped his seat belt on, I turned back onto the road, heading away from the train station and towards the highway.

"You look pale," I said, placing my palm on his forehead.

He swatted me away. "I'll be fine."

The sun was shining overhead, a few wisps of white streaked through the blue, and the road was open before us.

All the death hadn't quite caught up with me yet. Autopilot was engaged, and all I knew was one destination. The one we'd been aiming for all this time. Fortitude.

"Do you think the cops will come after us?" I asked, not liking the silence between us.

"I doubt it."

"We've left DNA and fingerprints clear across the country," I argued. "Haven't you ever seen that TV show *CSI*?"

"They had enough clout to seal off several cars of that train, Sloane. Believe me when I say, they're connected enough to clean up the trail of destruction we've left across the country...and that's not taking compulsion into consideration. The only people coming for us now are them."

"Ironically, that's extremely helpful," I drawled.

"They want this off the record."

"Who are *they*? I think I've earned the right to know the name of the vampires who've chased us clear across the country."

"They have a lot of names."

"Such as?"

"The Marauders. The Vanguard. The Hollow Men."

I snorted. "Are you serious?"

Chaser grunted. "Their leader is called The King."

"The King?" I scowled and tightened my grip on the wheel. "What kind of name is that?"

"Did they say anything while you were with them?"

I shrugged. "They said something about a sacrifice."

Chaser cursed. He knew...of course he did. I snorted and fixed my gaze on the road ahead. We had a six-hour drive ahead of us, so there was no use debating the supposed fate of daddy's little girl, or that would make for a tense ride to Fortitude. We hadn't even talked about the other thing. Us and...*her*.

"Pull over," Chaser demanded, startling me.

"What? Why? We've got to find you a warm body to counteract all that mummification...unless you want to drink from me." I shivered. "Maybe that's a little too personal."

"Sloane. *Stop*."

Sighing, I slowed the car and eased off the road. Stopping, I turned off the engine and stared out the front windscreen, listening to the sound of a truck whooshing past.

I wasn't sure I wanted to hear whatever he was going to say, either. After everything we'd been through on that train... Actually, I didn't want to know.

"I need to explain," he said.

Screwing my eyes shut, I held onto the wheel and said a silent prayer. I was already broken. I didn't need an explanation as to why he acted the way he did. He would only dump salt into the open wound.

"A century ago—"

"*No*," I snapped.

"If you want to survive, you need to understand all of it, Sloane."

I said nothing. I could feel Chaser's gaze burn into the side of my face and I began to tremble. *I should have stayed a wolf...*

"I worked with *them*," he said. "I knew them as the Hollow Men."

My mouth fell open, and I turned to stare at him. Another truck flew past, shaking the car, but I couldn't speak.

Chaser took out his wallet from the bag at his feet and slipped the photograph of the woman out of the soft leather. He stared at it, his expression twisting.

He sensed me staring and turned it over. Writing was scrawled over the back, that old-fashioned cursive that was impossible to read, but I could make out just enough to know it was a name and a date.

"Loretta," he said after a long moment. "Her name was Loretta."

I knew I was supposed to say something reassuring, but I didn't have it in me. I was frozen, completely numb. A pretty name to match her pretty face. He'd said it with such...*love.*

"I couldn't protect her anymore," he went on. "She saved my life, but I couldn't save hers." He lowered his gaze and slipped the photograph back into his wallet. "When I first turned, I was lost. I couldn't handle what I'd become, the things I'd done...so I turned it all off.

My humanity was in shreds. I'd made a name for myself by tearing through half of England, leaving a bloody trail behind me. A trail that the Hollow Men had picked up."

"They recruited you," I murmured.

Chaser nodded. "A decade passed...I came to Australia and more time passed, then I met her. Loretta." His hands shook and he ran them through his hair, his greying skin beginning to look more drawn. "She brought me back."

And the Hollow Men didn't like it. Chaser had his humanity, he was in love, and they couldn't control him anymore. He knew all their secrets, which meant he was a liability.

Chaser didn't have to fill in the blanks, I understood what had happened next.

My heart broke. "They took her, didn't they?"

"I was on the run..." His voice wavered. "I wanted to get her back before it was too late, but I had no one."

"So you went to Fortitude."

"They were the only supernaturals willing to go against the Hollow Men. The alpha saw the worth in my loyalty, no matter how he gained it. I knew his enemy inside and out. With my knowledge, he could finish them off for good. The wolves would help me get her back, but by the time we made our play, it was too late. They'd already killed her, but I'd already been bound." He held up his hand, showing me the crossed sword tattoo on his thumb. "Didn't matter if she was dead or alive, the pack had held up their end, and I was... What did you call it? Enslaved and branded?" He snorted and wiped his eyes. "This is my repayment. A magical brand that binds me to the pack for all time. When I said I didn't have a choice, I meant it, Sloane."

Oh, God. Of all the scenarios that had played in my mind, this was not one of them. His life had been brutally torn from him and now he was enslaved to my father and all the Fortitude alphas that'd came before.

"So, you turned it off again..." I whispered. He'd turned it off rather than feel the death of Loretta and the pain of the things Fortitude had forced him to do.

"You were right," he murmured. "I'm a criminal and a murderer. *Your father's dog.*"

"You were trying to get justice," I said. "You did what you thought needed to be done."

"I didn't expect you, Sloane."

I snorted, struggling to hold in my tears. I hadn't expected him, either.

He sighed and leaned back in the seat. "It's not easy letting her go."

"I can't make you do anything," I said, my throat burning with unshed tears—some of them selfish ones for myself, "but I can't play this game anymore. I won't."

"Sloane..."

"You can't give her up, I understand that. You can't help me because of that brand. I get it. That's why I need to walk away. I need to protect myself." The words struck deep in my heart, and it was all I could do to keep it together. "You need to get out of the car, Chaser."

"Sloane," he said, "you don't understand."

"I do. More than you realise."

His hand shot out and wrapped around my wrist. I struggled against his hold, but he was still stronger than I was, even with the blood loss.

"Get out," I snarled.

His iridescent eyes blazed, burning into mine like liquid fire. "*No.*"

I stared at him, completely lost.

"I feel things for you, Sloane," he murmured. "I don't know what they are, and I shouldn't have them, but I do." His breath hitched. "I will be the death of you, but... I'm a selfish bastard."

Chaser was asking me to stay, even though it meant going to Fortitude. He couldn't leave, his brand enslaved him to the alpha, *my father*. He was asking me to free him.

"Me?" I whispered, completely dumbfounded. "You're asking *me* for help?"

His eyes narrowed. "You're the one who made my humanity return. Call it payback."

"That explains the emotional whiplash." I shook my head. "How do you know?"

Chaser coughed and pressed the heel of his palm over his heart. "It was small things at first, then more and more. When a vampire turns off their emotions, who they were before is shut away. The onslaught of all the things they did while they were off flood in and overwhelm everything. Guilt, remorse, pain, longing… I'm not sure I can suffer a century of it without…" He coughed again and lowered his head. "I can't remember who I was."

And I didn't know who I was now that I'd turned. *What a pair we made.*

Turning in the seat, I held out my arm. "Here."

He looked at me, his brow creasing. "I can't."

"You need blood," I told him. "Take mine."

"Sloane, your blood is what this is all about. The blood of the wolf who can turn at will."

"They said there was supposed to be a sacrifice," I said. "I assume that's got to be some witchy thing and until then, it's just blood, right?"

His gaze flickered to my wrist. "I don't know."

"And if it's not? What will it do to you?"

"They believe your blood holds the key to true immortality," he replied. "A cure for all things that could kill them."

I screwed up my nose. "How do they figure that?"

"Because you are immune to the ultimate curse," Chaser explained. "You alone have control over your supernatural form. No wolf, no vampire, or even witch can choose between humanity and what they are. Only you."

I wasn't sure I understood how that equated to true

immortality—maybe it didn't—but they believed it and that's all that mattered.

"So, you better drink before you desiccate again," I told him, thrusting my wrist at him again. "All I can see are plusses."

Chaser looked torn for a moment, then he wrapped his fingers around my wrist. "This will sting."

I nodded. "Do what you have to."

He lowered his lips towards my wrist, his hazel eyes misting into blackness, and I grimaced as his fangs pierced my flesh.

I felt my blood leave my arm and my head spun as he drank. Leaning back against the seat, my eyes fluttered and I stared at him as he fed, completely transfixed. It was strangely erotic having his mouth on me, my blood returning him to life.

He sighed when he pulled away, sinking back against the passenger seat. The colour was returning to his cheeks, but I knew he hadn't drank enough, not by a long shot. The little he'd taken from me was just a stopgap until we found him something—*someone* —more.

"Do you feel any different?" I whispered as he pressed his thumb against a fang.

A drop of blood beaded on his torn flesh and he rubbed it into the bite mark on my wrist, even though my wolfness would probably heal me. Though, I appreciated the human gesture. *He did care.*

"No," he said. "I feel the same."

He let me go and I turned towards the road. Right now, we were on a dangerous precipice.

Nothing was solved. Nothing at all. My father was still after me, and so were the Hollow Men. Chaser and I were finally on the same page but...

"It was meant to be an easy job," he said. "I was given an address, a description, and a destination. Everything that happened after I first laid eyes on you..."

"Wasn't meant to happen," I finished.

"No."

"Way to make a girl feel special."

He smirked before sitting back in the seat. He looked exhausted and in no shape to make any coherent decisions, which meant I had to make them for us.

"I don't know why," he whispered. "I knew about who you were, that the vampires wanted you for your blood...and that rival packs want you dead. As for Fortitude? All he told me was that he wanted to keep you safe."

I scoffed, "Which means he wants me for something."

Thinking about the scenarios that had plagued me since our road trip began, I couldn't quite piece it together. Fortitude was in the middle of a war with the Hollow Men, which started a century ago. Chaser had noble intentions, wanting to rescue Loretta, but the wolves had seen an opportunity to grasp more power. Where did I fit into all this? Why was my blood so special to the vampires? *What's in it for Fortitude?*

There was only one way to find out.

"I want to go to Fortitude," I declared.

Chaser frowned and chewed on his bottom lip. After weeks of trying to convince him to run away with me, I'd just slapped him in the face.

"Why the sudden change of heart?"

"I want to see my father."

"After all we've been through?"

"What have they given you in a century?" I asked. "They tricked you into immortal slavery. They've made you do things I can't even wrap my mind around. My story doesn't have a happy ending...I know my father is lying. I'm not his daughter, I'm a commodity."

"Sloane, what are you saying?"

"One thing has become crystal-clear," I murmured. "After all the attempted murders, the kidnapping, the torture... After all the blood... He's not fit to be alpha."

Chaser stared at me, his expression changing so fast I couldn't keep up. It didn't matter what he thought at the end of this. All that mattered was the battle to come.

"I'm going to take it from him," I said, reaching over and turning the key in the ignition. "I'm going to make the Fortitude wolves mine, and he won't even see it coming. I will not be a pawn in his game, and you will never be a slave again."

His lips curved as the engine turned over and sparked to life.

"I have no idea what I'm doing, so I'm going to need help." I grasped his hand and met his gaze. "Are you with me?"

Chaser returned my grasp, threading his fingers through mine. "*Long live the queen.*"

OTHER BOOKS IN

THE FORTITUDE WOLVES TRILOGY...

Werewolves and vampires are embroiled in a war for supremacy and a troubled woman is in the centre of it all...only she doesn't know it.

Packed with suspense, action, and supernatural secrets, this series is sure to keep readers on the edge of their seats...

Wolf Called #1

Wolf Fated #2

Wolf Hunted #3

WOLF FATED
(Fortitude Wolves - Book Two)

Hunted by vampires. Challenging for alpha. For werewolf Sloane, the real battle is about to begin.

After being pursued by vampires and hunted by rival wolves, Sloane and Chaser have finally made it to their destination—the home of the Fortitude Wolves, the meanest werewolf pack on the east coast of Australia.

With vampires desperate to control her extraordinary power, Sloane is faced with a new challenge—how to understand who she was born to be —but there's only one thing she wants after all the misery she's been through. *A happy ending.* One where the Fortitude Wolves are hers to rule and her father's legacy is ash on the wind.

With Chaser by her side and one long list of people to avenge, she believes she can challenge for alpha and win, but earning the trust of the pack is easier said than done.

She's about to learn that supernatural loyalty is the most dangerous game of them all.

Wolf Fated is the second book in the Fortitude Wolves trilogy, a suspenseful Urban Fantasy series where werewolves and vampires go to war for the ultimate prize— true immortality.

ABOUT NICOLE

Nicole R. Taylor is an Australian Urban Fantasy author.

She lives in the western suburbs of Melbourne dreaming up nail biting stories featuring sassy witches, duplicitous vampires, hunky shapeshifters, and devious monsters.

She likes chocolate, cat memes, and video games.

When she's not writing, she likes to think of what she's writing next.

Follow Nicole Online:

Website: nicolertaylorwrites.com
Facebook: facebook.com/nrtaylorwrites
Newsletter: nicolertaylorwrites.com/newsletter

fraught with danger and forbidden romance... and the ultimate battle to save magic before it's gone forever.

THE DARKLAND DRUIDS - A woman with no living relatives travels from Australia to the other side of the world to find out the truth of who she is...only to land in the middle of a prophecy of destruction. Druids, witches, fae, and shapeshifters abound in this thrilling magical adventure!

Find out more at: NicoleRTaylorWrites.com

See what titles are FREE at: Nicole's Free Reads

9 781922 624253